THE *WHY NOT*

Victor J. Banis

The Borgo Press
An Imprint of Wildside Press

MMVII

CONTENTS

THE *WHY NOT*, by Victor J. Banis

FOREWORD

The Why Not was written in 1965 and first published in 1966—not an auspicious time for gay fiction. In 1963, in what was a *cause célèbre* for advocates of freedom of speech, Fresno publishers Sanford Aday and Wallace de Ortega Maxey were convicted of distributing obscene material and sentenced to 25 years in prison. The books for which they were convicted were tepid compared to the writings of, say, Mickey Spillane. It was their homosexual content, and that alone, that rendered them obscene—and that sent these publishers to prison; and sent a chill throughout the publishing word. At that moment, no one wanted to publish homosexual material.

Well, what did I know? I had already been through a lengthy trial of my own for conspiring to distribute obscene material—four months in a Sioux City, Iowa courtroom for a book, *The Affairs of Gloria*, that had one "damn" in it and one "go to hell." It did, however, significantly have some—again, tepid—lesbian scenes.

In for a penny, in for a pound. I wanted to write a gay novel, and write it I did, and it was my great good fortune that it reached the hands of Earl Kemp at Greenleaf Classics, who would be my chief editor for the next several years. Years later, Earl would say of *The Why Not*:

There were many thousand of paperback novels published under my direction (in the 60s,) and ninety-nine percent of them all started out as original manuscripts. There was

5

a point in time when we were almost inundated with unsolicited submissions by wannabe writers, the proverbial "slush pile." We also had a very good First Reader named Bill. It was his job to wade through all those novice manuscripts looking for passable material. His word was the first absolute final word in the whole editorial department

From those approximate 4,000 paperback titles that we published I can remember around four manuscripts only of truly significant worth, both as literature and as a viable portrayal of our liberated times. These are manuscripts that almost from the minute they arrived at the office began making ripples of excitement that flowed instantaneously from editor to editor.

Such a day happened when Bill opened the package containing the manuscript for *The Why Not*. He barely even began his customary quick-eyescan-and-quicker-rejection routine when something grabbed him and he stopped reading. When he realized that he didn't need to read the manuscript, he brought it directly into my office...the first time he had ever done any such thing. (Actually, office protocol dictated that he follow procedure, and pass anything to me through the editor in chief.)

"I think you need to look at this manuscript yourself," he told me.

And I did, and I agreed with Bill and I also recognized it was something remarkable, timely and apt to be rather popular. I bought that manuscript right then without even reading it all the way through and I've never regretted that decision for a moment.

I feel it was a pivotal book that opened doors too-long closed and one of the major

THE *WHY NOT*, by Victor J. Banis

building blocks in (the) ongoing fight for First Amendment realities.

* * * * * * *

 The Why Not did indeed open doors to gay writers, and, as Greenleaf's first gay novel (as well as mine) it is often credited with launching the gay publishing revolution that so changed the gay world in the '60s and '70s. It sold well for its publisher and got a glowing review in *Publishers Weekly* and an even better one from Joseph Hanson writing in *One Magazine*. I only regret that I do not have those reviews today, so that I could include them here. You will just have to take my word for them; but, if any of you should have them, I would be glad to hear form you.

 Over the years since its publication, the book has become a collector's item; an autographed copy was offered a year or so ago for $175.00—quite a rate of inflation, considering that the original sold for seventy-five cents—and I am routinely asked at book shows and other gatherings to sign copies for those collectors.

 The *Why Not* was modeled after an actual bar, The Castaways, on Commonwealth Avenue, and in its heyday, it was perhaps the most popular gay bar in Hollywood. Incidentally, it was my old friend, Elbert Barrow (who was the model for Lady Agatha in the book) who nicknamed it the Why Not. A typical Saturday afternoon exchange might go, "Are you coming to the bar tonight?" and the answer was usually, "Why not?"

 The last I saw, there was a Japanese karaoke bar where once The Castaways stood. The *Why Not* is long gone, but I am glad the old girl's stories linger on.

—Victor J. Banis

11:59 AM
Saturday Morning

◄Chapter One►

His body was very near mine, its warmth permeating the sheet that lay over us both.

"Are you there?" he asked, and I answered, "Yes."

In the semi-gloom of the bedroom, his hand reached out to touch mine, and our fingers clasped. "I thought that you had gone," he said. I said nothing, and held my breath, and wondered who he was.

My eyes turned in the other direction, unwilling to look upon him just yet, not until my thoughts became more lucid, not until I was ready to face a morning-stranger's face.

A clock stood on this side of the bed, safely within my range of vision. It was morning, then, Saturday morning; or rather, just barely morning; for between the small hand, pointing piously at twelve, and the big hand, there was only space enough for one tick of the mechanism. The shaft of black crouched, poised and tense, waiting to spring upon the dot marked twelve, and so end another morning in its tedious life.

Saturday morning came after Friday night, and Friday night was a time for the *Why Not*, for drinks that lasted long into the night and, hopefully, a rendezvous with passion that lasted well into the morning.

THE *WHY NOT*, by Victor J. Banis

So then, it was not so unusual this noon—now that the hour had struck—to find myself in a strange bed, hearing a strange voice, my hand still clasped in unfamiliar, urgent fingers.

I stirred finally, turning on my back, and saw the mirror crudely attached to the ceiling, my own likeness scowling down at me, a solemn jury of self-examination. Turning further, toward him, trying to focus my sleep-weary eyes. A wave of golden hair rippled over the pillow near me, too near to see really well. A face watched me with something almost frightening in its expression: a half smile, meant perhaps to be friendly, or seductive, and succeeding in neither goal. It was not a bad face, this collection of eyes, nostrils and swollen lips that lay in front of me. I had seen worse, at closer range. On Saturday mornings, especially, I had seen worse.

He waited, no doubt studying me in the same surreptitious way in which I studied him. My lips automatically smiled, a reflex action, my eyes half-closing as I edged closer to the face, sought the swollen lips. His breath was sour and unpleasant, tasting of cigarettes and stale booze, his mouth less yielding than one would have liked; his body, molding itself now to mine, was rather too soft. Obediently, mechanically, my sex hardened, reaching out and up for him, seeking its prey.

Tonight, I told myself, tonight I would go again to the *Why Not*; seek another face to find on my pillow the following morning. But for now, the long empty afternoon stretched before me, a wasteland of time and tedium, and here, for the moment, was an oasis of relief.

THE *WHY NOT*, by Victor J. Banis

* * * * * * *

By day, the *Why Not* was not so much depressing as dull, a building lacking in its exterior any trace of character or expression. Its front, painted red—but a lazy red, not one of those lively, hot shades—crowded rudely against the sidewalk, glaring petulantly at the street before it, pushing itself against the Laundromat on one side and the empty storefront on the other. It might have been a convenient stopping-off spot for the men of the neighborhood except that, during the day it remained stubbornly, snobbishly closed. Like its patrons, the bar was a nighttime creature.

Under the cover of darkness, however, even its faded exterior took on a new charm, the dull red reflecting the glow of the aged neon that proclaimed its name, the door curtained but congenially open to the stream of young men—and so rarely, women—who hurried in, leaving behind the darkened street to be caught up in the swell and flow of the crowds within. At night, on almost any night, the crowds were vast, shuffling feet blotting out the uneven, sawdust-covered floor, littered with cigarette butts, matchbook covers, sometimes dropped and unnoticed money; and, too often, discarded dreams.

The counter of the bar itself was packed, a shabby wedge of flypaper littered with swarming bodies that leaned on it, stood before it, sometimes sat on it. It was not so much a room as a cloud of flesh and faces. The faces caught the glow from the strands of lights, tiny Japanese bulbs confiscated from some forgotten chest of Christmas ornaments

11

to be hung about the ceiling and posts without apparent pattern or purpose.

There were mirrors, too, that caught and multiplied the faces—one stood smiling at a stranger who proved after all to be only oneself smiling back—and a bit of netting which, together with a cluster of dusty artificial leaves, was intended to create a Polynesian effect. An embarrassed and self conscious décor that was, at the same time, inherently right, so unreal in itself that it lent an air of reality to the moods and the people contained within the room.

* * * * * * *

"Glory be, he is alive."

Lon blinked his eyes once or twice before finally squinting in the direction of the voice. He tried to smile responsively, although he found the remark rather unfunny. That was not an unusual fact. He found most things unfunny when he had just awakened.

"I had all but concluded you were dead," Jackie went on, ignoring the ill-fated attempt at a smile. "Do you want coffee?"

Jackie was already dressed, obviously had been up for quite a while. The ashtray, perched precariously atop one pillow, was filled to the brim with cigarette stubs, one of them still smoldering.

"Love some," he said. "You smoke too much."

"I do everything too much. I never hear you complain about the sex." This was delivered from the kitchen, over the clatter of cup and saucer.

12

THE *WHY NOT*, by Victor J. Banis

"Depends on what you call too much. Some things should be excessive, you know."

He kicked the covers lazily aside, stretching his six-foot frame taut, and smiled more successfully as a lingering lethargy reminded him of the night's activities.

"God, you're obscene," Jackie declared, returning to the room with the coffee.

"I'm hung, if that's what you mean," he retorted with a leer and a glance downward.

"Umm-hum." The coffee cup descended with a bang to the nightstand. "You butch bastards are all alike. You think we can't see your naked bodies without getting all hot and bothered."

"Can you?" Lon reached, pulled the lithe young body down to the bed. The lips that met his were warm and eager.

"Get out of here," Jackie snapped, pushing against his chest, although with a teasing smile. "You've already slept half the day away. If you want to waste all that time, that is your privilege, but I have things to do this afternoon."

Lon frowned and released his hold, scooting to a sitting position. "You know, if we didn't have to wait half the night to get started, I wouldn't sleep all day."

Jackie's eyebrows lifted in a warning gesture. "Don't start. You know my evenings aren't free. I have to think of Lindy."

"I'll say you do." Lon's tone was one of genuine annoyance now. "I don't know why you two don't just go on and get married. Lindy, all the time, Lindy."

"Lon, Lindy has done so much for me...."

13

THE *WHY NOT*, by Victor J. Banis

"Shit!"

Jackie sighed, abandoning the explanation as a bad attempt and reached instead for another cigarette. "You are in a temper this morning, aren't you?"

Lon studied the youthful creature seated on the edge of the bed—tiny, little-boyish—someone who did not know from experience would never suspect the fiery passions hidden beneath that innocent façade. He met the soft, limpid eyes and his anger diminished.

"Sorry," he grunted, pulling his lover close again in an affectionate embrace.

They kissed, affection quickly turning to arousal as Lon responded to the close warmth. "Breakfast?" he asked with a wink.

"Oh, you!" Jackie pulled away again and stood, reaching to flip the covers over the distracting nakedness. "I should have been out of here an hour ago."

Lon pushed the covers stubbornly away again, smiling confidently. "It can't be that much of a hurry, can it?" He stretched, tightening his muscles, his erection a physical witness to his state of mind.

He watched the eyes, knowing that he had won the argument as they grew brighter. He held out a hand in invitation.

Jackie's scowl became a smile, resigned and pleased all at once. Lon watched eagerly as the white sweater was pulled upward and off, the black slacks pushed downward and off. He opened his arms, welcoming the pale, warm body to his own.

THE *WHY NOT*, by Victor J. Banis

* * * * * * *

Later, Jackie rose and dressed again, hurrying and stealing frequent glances at the clock. "I feel like a stripper in a three-shows-a-night club—on again, off again, on again."

Lon, smugly satisfied now, remained in bed, sipping his lukewarm coffee contentedly.

"Tell you what," Jackie offered, standing over him again when the ritual of dressing was completed, "How about we spend an evening together, a whole evening? Would that make you happy?"

Lon snorted his disbelief. "I won't hold my breath," he said, "Lindy owns your evenings, sugar, Lindy and that damned bar."

"It's not that damned bar, it's the *Why Not*. Besides, I mean it. I'll ask Lindy to get someone to work tonight. I'll tell him I am sick. I am, really, I'm sick of working all the time. I haven't had a night off in months."

"How in the hell did you two get stuck with that place, anyway?"

Jackie shrugged. "We wanted it. Anyway, it's doing all right now, really, it's making money. If business keeps up, we can hire someone to run it before too long. Then I won't be so tied up all the time."

"There will still be Lindy. He won't relinquish your time so easily."

Jackie sighed and said nothing. It was a familiar argument.

"Does he know about us?"

Jackie's head shook slightly. "Not really, not all about us. He knows I see you from time to time. He thinks we're just buddies."

Lon snorted again. Jackie seemed about to say something more, but did not. "I have got to run."

"Comb your hair," Lou snapped after the retreating figure.

Jackie laughed and paused before the mirror on the wall, running a comb hurriedly through the short, tousled auburn hair. There was a final smile, a kiss blown from across the room, and Lon was left alone.

* * * * * * *

John Branloe lighted a cigarette, noticing at the same time the one already smoldering in the ashtray in front of him. He looked from one to the other and finally extinguished the shorter of the two before he stood and beginning to pace the room.

The room was a lovely one, high-ceilinged and generous of proportion, its all-too-fine furnishings expertly placed in decorous groupings. In the gold-framed mirror over the fireplace, Branloe studied his own, worried face. It was time. His guest, or rather his caller, was late. "Probably," he reminded himself, "Wants to make me sweat."

"If he's too late," he mumbled with some concern, "Mary will be here." The thought only made him more nervous and he stubbed out the only half-smoked cigarette in another ashtray. "If she is home when he comes, I won't let the little bastard in the door," he promised himself. "That will teach him a lesson."

He looked out the window for the fifth time, saw nothing in the drive and, with a muttered oath, went to the bar and poured himself a drink. It was a rotten, lousy business anyway, that was his opinion of it. He should not even have talked to the little son-of-a-bitch when he called. Well, that could not be helped, since he had answered the phone himself. But he could have given him a good earful, and he should have. Why in the name of anyone had he agreed to see him? Worse yet, told him to come to the house? It was bad enough as it was, without having that little faggot swishing in and out of his house.

The drink was having its effect, though, calming his nerves somewhat and replacing his tension in part with indignation and anger. What if he just refused to see him when he got here? What could the little punk do? All his threats about whom he would talk to and what he would say—what did they really amount to anyway, but a lot of hot air? All that had been a long time ago, at least a couple of years back, when Mary was in Europe with her mother. Hell, at least he had not been whoring around with other women, the way some men did— well, at least not to any extent. One or two, maybe, but Mary had been gone for better than three months. You could not expect a man to do nothing for that long.

But it was not as though he had gone out looking for anything. Even that damned fairy had come to him, come to a party with someone (try though he might, he could not remember or find out

17

whom he had come with.) But he had been there, and he had taken after old John like a house afire.

Hell, what was wrong with it? If some silly faggot wanted to give you a good time and you had been doing without for a while, what was the harm in giving him a few good minutes? Ten lousy minutes, twenty at the most; how important could it be in a man's life? It had been one-sided, that was for sure. Maybe he had tried to be polite, but you could not blame anybody for that. Hell, the kid was there, working up a sweat to give him a good time. There wasn't anything wrong in trying to be nice and trying to reciprocate. And the fact that he definitely had not liked it was proof enough that old John was not queer.

For a moment he remembered it, the way it had been, just the two of them together, eager for fulfillment—but he pushed that thought stubbornly from his mind. Okay, so maybe he had enjoyed it a little. Who didn't like getting his rocks off? But that did not make him queer, and nobody, including that damned faggot, could say that he was.

Two thousand lousy bucks! He'd given him four times that much already!

Despite his bravado, however, he jumped when the doorbell rang. He set the drink on the coffee table, neglecting to place a coaster under it to protect the marble, and hurried toward the door. The maid, thank God, was in the back. There was no need for her even to see who was here, unless she got to snooping around.

"If I catch that Mexican snooping," John swore to himself, "I will fire her in a minute. That will teach her a lesson."

18

THE *WHY NOT*, by Victor J. Banis

It was him, all right. Nicky, leaning casually against a pillar and smiling that lopsided smile.

He ought to be a girl, John Branloe thought as he opened the door. Yeah, he would make a good-looking girl, all right. If he was a girl, I would take him on in a minute.

"You're late," he snapped, holding the door open. He was not going to try to be polite to the little bastard. "My wife might be home any minute."

Nicky laughed, his voice unpleasantly shrill, and wriggled his way past John into the hall. "You are such a fusspot," he teased, his eye taking in the corridor in one sweep. "You told me on the phone she doesn't get home till after two. We've got time for all kinds of fun, if you want. What a lovely home!" All of this was said in one breath, without pause or expression. It might have been a recording, a mechanical creature who was speaking, but for the flamboyant movements of his hands and the constant shifting of his gaze.

"I do not like you coming here," John snapped, stubbornly ignoring the invitation. "You know better than that. I told you not even to call here."

"How was I to reach you, sweetie?" Nicky was the picture of malicious innocence as he ambled down the hall, John following meekly. "Your nasty secretary keeps telling me you're out when I call the bank. I was beginning to think you were avoiding me, although I know that is positively silly—is this the living room?"

Without waiting for an invitation or even an answer, he entered the living room, continuing to examine his surroundings with a swift but calculat-

19

ing eye. "Got a drink for me, sweetie?" he asked abruptly, catching sight of the half-full glass on the table.

"What is this about money?" John asked, swearing to himself that he was not going to serve this little fairy a drink. He would see him dry up first and turn to dust.

"I need another loan, silly, that's all," Nicky explained. He crossed the room as he spoke, examined the bottles on the bar, and poured himself a glass of the best Scotch. "I thought I explained all that to you on the phone."

"A loan?" John snorted indignantly. They had all been loans and he had not seen one penny of it being paid back. And he never would, that much he felt sure of. "I haven't got that kind of money. I can't run around handing it out to anybody and everybody."

He was sweating, nervous again. He dropped into the chair nearest him and reached across the table for his drink.

"That is too bad," Nicky told him, coming back across the room to perch on the arm of the chair. His hand went out and made its way lightly through John's thinning hair, disarranging it. "Maybe if I waited around and we talked to your wife when she comes home...."

John was shaking now, the ice cubes in his glass rattling loudly. He was over a barrel. The little punk would be dirty enough to do just what he threatened. How had he gotten into this, anyway, all over a little sex? Just because he had been too drunk to say no, and Nicky had pushed it. Had taken advantage of him, really.

THE *WHY NOT*, by Victor J. Banis

He set his drink on the table, painfully aware of the slender body close to his; close enough to smell the flowery, too-sweet perfume. A woman's perfume, damn him! John closed his eyes and swallowed, trying to remove the bad taste in his mouth.

"I don't have the money here," he whispered hoarsely. "I can't get it until later today."

"That is too bad," Nicky crooned, his hand tracing a pattern now over John's neck. "You will just have to bring it to me tonight, then, won't you? Unless you want me to wait here for it?"

"I'll bring it," John agreed, wishing Nicky would stop whatever he was doing with his hand. "It'll be around ten, okay?"

"You are so sweet to me," Nicky murmured, setting his drink aside to devote both his hands to his ministrations.

I'm getting hot, John was thinking, not without agony. I am getting all worked up over this crappy punk. Christ, if only Mary was here! I would rather have a woman any time. Nothing like that to cure what ails you—not like with some two-bit queer. I wish he would take his hands off me, quit feeling around.

"Let's go to the bathhouse," he whispered finally, pleading. I'm just horny, he told himself, trying to still the voices shouting within him. There is nothing wrong with that, he thought, as long as nobody finds out.

Nicky smiled without pretense as he stood and allowed John to rise from the chair. Not that he wanted the fat old man—all shriveled up, like he had been soaked in vinegar. I wonder how his wife stays awake, he thought idly, and chuckled to him-

21

self. For the same reasons I feel him up and give him a good time, he told himself. After all, poor silly John is so rich, and so scared of scandal, scared of what those silly men at the bank would think if they found out. It sure did make a girl's life easier, having jerks like old John around.

Two thousand bucks. If the old fool wasn't horny when he brought the money around, little Nicky could get rid of him early and still have time to run over to the *Why Not*. Wouldn't those dizzy queens take notice when they saw he had money again! And that snotty Jackie, damn bitch. That one would be sweet as sugar for a change.

"Go to hell, Mary," he would say to anyone who got smart with him.

Oh, it's going to be a wild Saturday night, he thought with glee.

* * * * * * *

Freddie stood at the door of the apartment and watching his young trick of the night before cross the street and climb into a car, an old Ford, nothing too exciting. He returned the final wave before closing the door, without waiting for him to drive away. In his hand he held a scrap of paper, the trick's phone number. Doug, was that his name? For a brief moment Freddie stared down at the slip of paper, torn from an old bridge score pad. Then, sadly, almost reverently, he crumpled it up and dropped it into an ashtray on his way to the kitchen. He never liked repeats. He passed the mirror on his way. One quick glance was all he needed to tell him that he looked like hell.

THE *WHY NOT*, by Victor J. Banis

In the kitchen, Walt was just pouring himself a cup of coffee. Good old Walt, so comfortable, the proverbial pair of old shoes, smiling a good morning at him.

"Nice," Walt greeted him, taking a second cup from the cupboard and pouring coffee for Freddie. "Where did you pick him up?"

"The *Why Not*," Freddie answered, accepting the coffee and seating himself across the small breakfast table from Walt. "Someone Jackie introduced me to. Christ, am I beat. What a night."

He started to go on, wanting to tell someone about the supple, inexhaustible young stud who had just left, but he caught himself, recognizing the fleeting hurt in Walt's eyes before he looked down into his coffee cup. He had forgotten, again, his promises to himself to be more thoughtful; had forgotten, again, that Walt was still hopelessly in love with him.

His remorse, however, was short-lived, followed by a moment of petty annoyance. We are only roommates, he told himself angrily. He reminded himself in the next moment that it had not always been so. But that was three years ago, now—three years since they had been lovers. That should be long enough for Walt to forget. But it hadn't been, obviously, he was all too aware of that fact. Not that anything was ever said. Walt was too kind for that, too loyal.

Maybe, Freddie thought, and it was a familiar thought, maybe I should move out. It would be kinder to him, and easier for me. But this present arrangement was Walt's idea. It had been his suggestion, when their relationship as lovers ended, that they remain friends instead, roommates.

I will just have to move, Freddie told himself, knowing even as he thought it that he wouldn't move. It was too comfortable with Walt, too secure—always someone there, the coffee brewed in the morning, a fast loan if money ran short, which was often, a car to borrow, a sure companion if one was needed.

Face it, he thought, you take advantage of his feelings for you. On the other hand, of course, you could not take advantage of someone who would not let you. If the relationship was unhealthy, there were two of them in it, certainly.

"What did you do last night?" he asked aloud, pushing the familiar subject from his mind. He had been thinking the same things for three years now. There was no urgent need for a solution just at this moment.

Walt shrugged, looked almost guilty, as though he had been found out in some wicked game. "Oh, nothing much," he said. "Watched a little television, wrote a letter home, went to bed early. Nothing very exciting. Not like your night was, obviously."

Freddie lit a cigarette, coughing as the harsh smoke poured into his throat. "That's the trouble with you," he said, "Staying home by yourself, going to bed at nine o'clock. On a Friday night, too. You should get out more, go to the bars."

Walt grimaced, helped himself to a cigarette from Freddie's pack, and leaned toward the match Freddie lit for him.

THE *WHY NOT*, by Victor J. Banis

"I don't see where that would get me," he said. "I would just spend too much money, and I would get up with a hangover the next morning, and I'd be no better off for it all."

"You might find a trick, for one thing." He regretted it when he had said it, annoyed by the plaintive, little-dog look that Walt gave him. Christ, *that* look. How often had he seen that.

"I'm not looking for anyone," Walt said simply, his sincerity an accusation that was far more effective than anger.

"Well, it might do you some good, just the same," Freddie answered curtly, irritated at being required to face such conversation so early in the day. Damn it, he knows I don't like to be annoyed when I've just gotten up.

Walt stood, refilling his cup, and remained at the window for a time, staring at the diminutive back yard. "I found an apartment," he said finally.

Freddie stubbed out his cigarette, blowing the smoke slowly through his nostrils. "Not again," he groaned, definitely irritated now. This was the third time in one year. They were always moving; never done with boxes and crates and vans and rented trailers. Walt went through apartments the way some people went through lovers, never content for long with any of them. "We haven't been in this place for three months, even."

"I just don't like this place," Walt snapped, defensive now and annoyed also. "I told you that before."

"You liked it well enough when we rented it," Freddie said. Later, when he had calmed down, he would hate himself for arguing like this. He hated

25

scenes, hated discord of any sort. "I am sick to the gills of all this moving. And you have always got a reason, damn it, Walt. Can't you just stay settled in one place for a while?"

"It's a one bedroom," Walt said simply, not turning from the window. "The place I found."

Freddie caught himself, about to say something more. What did he mean by that—a one bedroom? Maybe, of course, he was hoping they could share a bed; that things might happen again between them...."We can't take a one bedroom, you know that," he said. "There isn't enough room here as it is, without trying to...."

"I was planning on moving by myself," Walt told him quickly, turning now to face Freddie.

It came like a blow, and for several minutes Freddie sat stunned and let the information sink into his consciousness. Walt had beaten him to it after all, the very thing he had been telling himself he would do. But he wasn't ready for it. It was just too sudden.

"I didn't mean to tell you like this," Walt went on, speaking hurriedly, his voice begging for understanding. "It's something I have been thinking about for a while. I think it might...well, it might be better, for both of us."

Freddie nodded his head, not so much agreeing as just answering. Breaking it up, getting separate apartments? But I can't live alone, he wanted to say. I have to have someone, someone to come home to, something to cling to. I need you here when I get back from the *Why Not* and I haven't found anybody. I can't even make a good pot of coffee by myself.

26

THE *WHY NOT*, by Victor J. Banis

"I don't mean we shouldn't still be friends," Walt was saying, still watching for some reaction. "I think the world of you, you know that. But it's hard for both of us this way. I don't like...well, I don't like a lot of things you do, all these bars and tricks, a new one every night or so. And it would be better for you to have a little more privacy. You need to be on your own for a while. You're not a kid any more, you know; neither of us is."

Freddie lit another cigarette, still nodding his head in time to some unheard music. "You're right, I guess," he said, not believing it at all. "I really do need to get out on my own."

"I'll help you find a place," Walt told him, relieved by Freddie's agreement, pleased that the argument had gone no further. "I won't be moving until the end of the month. If you need some money, I can help you with a little of the rent for a while."

"No, no, that's all right," Freddie assured him, getting up to pour himself another cup of coffee. "I'll manage."

How, he asked himself. How? How? How?

* * * * * * *

Lady Agatha flushes the john and stands, pulling his shorts up over his wide hips. He pauses, examining himself in the mirror. *Why can't I be hung* he thinks, instinctively clasping his inadequate genitals in his hand? He leaves his shorts down about his hips and pirouettes, peering over his shoulder. Nice fanny, something to be thankful for. Getting a little plump, however. (This is a sugar pill much relied on. He has always been plump, never

27

unpleasingly so.) They may say the closer the bone the sweeter the meat, but lots of men, she is well aware, prefer a little meat on the bone. Not the crew cut all-American ones, as a rule, they're always looking for the high school cheerleader; but the Latin types, now they go for a girl with some flesh.

She sighs, remembering a group of Spanish sailors—that was in Long Beach, and more years past than she wants to remember. Oh, they were sweethearts, with their oily, garlic-scented bodies and their inexhaustible passion. How many of them had there been? She makes as though to remember, although in fact she has since cherished the night in its every detail. Four of them—no, five—and just her and one other queen. God, how they burned up that beach, flinging themselves about in the sand— sand in her hair, sand in her shoes, sand in her drawers—sand, sand, sand. That had been a time.

Satisfied now that her derriere is still rea- sonably in shape, she pulls the skimpy Jockey shorts up and washes her hands. Must be sanitary, after all, she tells herself. Silly, the things a girl will have in her mouth in one night, and then worry about wash- ing her hands after going to the bathroom…but then, convention…she sighs at the burden of convention, although in truth it is a burden she has rarely deigned to bear

Finally, finished with the bathroom for the moment, she picks up the telephone from the floor where it is sitting, its long cord trailing after it, and carries it with her to the bedroom, glancing at the clock. Twenty minutes she sat in there, and not one phone call. Damn queens, too lazy to pick up the phone and dial a number.

THE *WHY NOT*, by Victor J. Banis

She sits on the edge of the bed, scratching in the vicinity of her crotch, and tries to think of someone to call. Larry, that bitch, will be in bed, no doubt. Him and his chicken. One of these days, Lady Agatha assures herself, he will get caught with some chicken, and they will haul that one away for a long rest. Do her good, too.

She frowns as she remembers a party at which Larry, who was with a perfectly nice boy himself, literally snatched a sweet young trick away from under her very nose. She could still see Larry smiling that bitchy smile of his afterward.

She makes a mental note to call Larry, but not now—tomorrow morning, maybe, nine o'clock or so. That will burn her, getting her out of bed before the Pope on a Sunday. This decision, however, leaves her still in doubt as to whom to call.

Well, it's not as though Larry is the only queen in this city. She flips open an address book on the table beside her and thumbs through it. Jackie, the little-sister-of-us-all? No, that one wouldn't be up either, not after working all night at that stinking bar. She thumbs on, smiling finally, then replaces the book and dials the phone, waiting impatiently for an answer.

Sweet little Ralph, always such a ball of fun—or at least he was until he got married, anyway. Not that Joe wasn't a sweetheart, sexy thing, and all that. I could have had him myself, she remembers—which is not at all true, since she made a pass at him one night in the restroom of the *Why Not* and he offered a polite but firm turndown. But Lady Agatha remembers that he begged her, right there with people swishing in and out of that stinking

29

place. Sweet little Ralph needn't think he got himself a virgin.

Not that they aren't a lovely couple. They go together rather nicely, as a matter of fact, blond and dark, tall and short. But they are so dull, now that they are settled down. Silly why people have to give up fun, just because they're not cruising any more.

She giggles at that thought: not cruising! Give either of them a sailor in tight pants with a bulge showing and they'd go out of their fruit minds. Dizzy queens, trying to act so pure...why the hell don't they answer their phone? She wonders as she half listens to the ring of the phone in her ear, what it would be like if she were married; but this is only the lingering ghost of an almost forgotten and long since abandoned dream.

"Hello?" Ralph. Had to be him, with that question mark in his voice.

"How are you, sweets?" Lady Agatha croons, giving her crotch a gentle pat. Almost without waiting for the polite answer, she begins to talk again. "Oh, I have had such a bitchy day. You know that Clara had a party last night, the sow, and didn't invite us...oh, you were invited?"

A pause, waiting to see if further information will be volunteered. When it was not, she went on, "Did you go? Well, I don't blame you. I wouldn't have gone if I had been invited. Clara's parties are always deadly dull. Anyway, she called me—let's see, it must have been nine o'clock, because I had just finished washing the dishes and I remember the news coming on as I drained the sink. Of course, I didn't tell her what I thought, never let on that I knew anything about her stinking party. Up her ass, that's what I say. She wanted to know if I could go shopping with her this afternoon, so I said yes, and she'll be by in about an hour to pick me up. And wouldn't you know, I saw the most gorgeous hunk of man standing outside, on the sidewalk, he was standing there the whole time I talked to her, and could I get that faggot off the telephone long enough to run outside and cruise it? Not on your life! Oh, God, basket to his knees, I swear it, and so obviously wanting someone to take him on."

Never once, as her monologue continues, does it occur to Lady Agatha that her listener might not be interested. After all, doesn't she call every day and recite, in great detail, everything—which is usually nothing—that has befallen her? And if it is of interest to her, it certainly should be of interest to her friends, as she saw it.

"Are you two coming out tonight?" she asks finally, interrupting herself in the middle of a sentence the idea of which she has forgotten.

"Ummm, I don't know, I'll have to check with Joe," Ralph said.

She's hedging. Agatha glowers viciously at the telephone. "Now don't go giving me a stall," she warns, playful in tone. "This is the fifth time I have called to invite you two for a drink, and I will take no excuses."

It is, in reality, the third time, but she remains certain that they won't remember. As though they even care, she thinks bitterly. And here I am, their very best friend.

"The *Why Not*?" Ralph asks after a pause.

"Why not?" Agatha quips in return. "About the witching hour?"

31

"That's fine."

Returning the receiver to its cradle, she contemplates whom else to call. Discovering that it is later than she thought, she jumps up and begins rummaging through the closets for something to wear. Clara will be here any second, and here she is, not even dressed.

Dressing does not, after all, take more than a few minutes. The make-up takes longer, standing until her legs ache before the mirror over the dresser. Finally, satisfied with the result, she gives a final upward brush of her hand to her lashes, darker and more delicately curved than before, and leans intently toward the mirror.

Oh, how did fairies get on without make-up, she wonders? Of course her eyes are outstanding even without anything on them, but how much more glamorous they are now. A good figure is one thing, and big meat is definitely an asset, but a pair of eyes—one could say anything with one's eyes, couldn't one?

The chime of the doorbell interrupts her self-contemplation. The clock near the bed tells her it is three-thirty, time for Clara—Clarence, if one must be butch—to be here. A final perusal of her makeup, and Agatha leaves the bedroom, swooping down upon the waiting door and her visiting "sister."

"Clara, you old bitch, you look lovely," she screams, flinging the door open and stretching out her arms for an embrace.

"Agatha, you have never looked better!" They squeal and embrace as though they had not met in years, although in fact it has been only a few days, not even a week. Like two old hens, they pick and fluff at one another, Agatha leading Clara into the parlor (so she calls it.)

"Where were you last night?" Clara demands, and Agatha widens her already too large eyes and says, "The *Why Not*. Why do you ask?"

"I thought you would be at my party, is why," Clara says, and Agatha, the epitome now of innocence, exclaims, "Party? Did you have a party last night?"

"You know perfectly well I did," Clara says "Not two days ago I asked you to come. On the phone, don't you remember?"

"Of course, of course! You know, it completely slipped my mind," Agatha declares, although in truth she remembers no such invitation. It is possible that she has forgotten. On the other hand, Clara, being the bitch she is, might be simply trying to make up. "Well, what a pity I didn't make it. I suppose that awful Ralph and his new husband, what is that one's name, Joe? I suppose they were there. Such a drag, those two. Calling me all the time, talking my ear off, Ralph does, and never anything to say. I let him talk me into meeting them tonight at the *Why Not*, of all things, for a drink. Can you imagine anything duller?"

Still fluttering, Clara admits that she can imagine nothing duller than meeting Ralph and Joe for a drink, and the two prepare for their shopping expedition, already arguing over which stores they should visit.

* * * * * * *

THE *WHY NOT*, by Victor J. Banis

Mid-afternoon—the day dragging slowly by. An hour or more with the golden boy, an hour not so much pleasant as existent. If only he had been more butch, I might have enjoyed sex that way. But for that I liked them butch. Nothing exciting about a soft, feminine queen—better that I had taken that role, groaning and pretending ecstasy, gaining some pleasure from the knowledge that his groans were real at least, a result of the pain I was inflicting.

And afterward, the interminable cup of coffee, dragging into an eternity of trivial exchange and futile attempts at camaraderie. The offered lift, declined, and the search for a bus stop, determining location and route. Halfway home now, one more bus to catch.

It was like sex with pillows. Why did they all turn out that way? They looked like people when you met them. I didn't recall meeting this one—it *had* been drunk out last night—but he must have seemed to be a person. They always did. Why did they all turn out to be stuffed animals?

Watching, cruising the boy coming down the street. He is young, virginal looking, probably a tourist. He glanced back—a good sign. Nice body, slender, firm, nice showing. Sweet looking, too, seventeen, eighteen maybe. Hell of an age to be gay. Too young for the bars, nothing to do but wander around on the streets, wishing you knew how to cruise, wondering why all the people cruising you pass you up. Not realizing that it's your age that scares them off. Except for the chicken queens, and they could be risky, they get scared when it's over, and sometimes they panic.

THE *WHY NOT*, by Victor J. Banis

He's cruising for sure, or wanting to, any-way—a quick glance, then looking away, stopping at that store window as though he were interested in antiques. Gorgeous behind—wouldn't you love to get into that? Maybe. Hopefully.

I could talk to him, make it easier. But instead I wait, without knowing why—afraid, maybe, of the age. He's shuffling, fidgeting, and I can all but hear his thoughts banging around in his head, running into each other. He's trying to think of something, the right thing, to say. Try "hello," I tell him si-lently; or smile a little.

Maybe he is not cruising, or maybe he's green, doesn't know yet what he really wants. That type is dangerous, the first to scream when they get it, or they go home and tell Momma that they are in love and I've got the men in blue banging at my door.

The bus coming into sight now, around the curve, looming down on us. It's the only one for hours; not many busses this way. I could take a cab. Ten dollars in my wallet; it would take half of that to get home.

He is smiling now. He has thought of it, whatever he means to say. Leaving the store win-dow, coming toward me. Should I step back? Let the bus pass and take a chance?

But he is not so pretty after all, up close: too many teeth. So young—they're always silly, and harder than anything to get rid of when you get tired of them.

"Hello," he says, hands deep in his pockets. Nice bulge, probably carries on like a mink.

THE *WHY NOT*, by Victor J. Banis

"Hi," in return, as I mount the steps to the bus. Maybe he'll catch it too, come along with me. But he doesn't. Still standing there when I look back, watching me in the window of the bus as I pull away, disappear finally.

* * * * * * *

Nearly colliding with an elderly woman, Jackie charged through the lobby of the shabby medical building, out the creaking door, and half walked, half ran across the parking lot to the waiting MG. Once safely inside the car there was a pause to light a cigarette and ponder over the news that had just been received.

Not news, really, so much as confirmation. Doctor Carter was correct, of that there was no doubt. Jackie had been certain before even making the appointment.

"Well, it's not the end of the world." The statement, made aloud, had a calming effect. It was true, there were things that could be done. After all, that had been the reason for choosing Doctor Carter. He wasn't even a particularly good MD, but he had a name among the gay set. All the boys came to him with their problems—"catching something" was a common ailment—and whether he was gay himself or not, he was known to be sympathetic. That was important to a gay man.

So it could be taken care of, one way or the other. But it was a nuisance and it certainly interfered with the plans for Lon. Lon would have to know, of course, although it was not a very pleasant matter to bring up. He would be angry. Dear Lon,

36

these days it seemed like he was always angry about something.

Jackie sighed and flipped the cigarette out of the car, reaching for the ignition key. A moment later, the MG roared out of the parking lot, nearly sideswiping an overweight Buick sedan, and headed in the direction of Silver Lake.

Lindy was already home. Ignoring his annoyed frown, Jackie gave him a loud, hasty kiss before hurrying into the kitchen and pouring a glass of milk.

"I hope that's not all you've eaten today," Lindy said, following behind.

"Oh, no, I had breakfast earlier." It wasn't really untrue, after all. You could consider Lon breakfast. Lots of the boys would be happy to start their day that way. "Oh, I need the evening off."

Lindy stared for a moment before shaking his head. "Don't be funny," he said. "Mike's out of town and Dick's in bed with the flu. I can't watch the place by myself, on a Saturday night."

"But I'm not feeling well either. Anyway, I haven't had a night off in ages."

"Neither have I," Lindy said. "And you don't look sick."

"This is important," Jackie insisted, pouting between swallows of milk

"No doubt," Lindy answered sarcastically. He turned and left the room. Jackie trailed after him.

"You could take a night off next week and I'll run the bar.

"You'd run us out of business, the way you give drinks away. Damn it, we're just getting the bar going, Jackie. Don't you ever think about all the work we've put into the place? I want to make a go of it, for your sake as well as mine...."

Jackie's eyes rolled heavenward. The lecture had started. It would last for quite some time, and in the end, Lindy would have his way, and Lon...oh, dear, Lon would be furious.

* * * * * * *

The solitary cowboy sits astride his horse and peers for a soulful moment into the vast horizon of the Western plains. Then, his eyes ablaze with emotions vaster than the setting, he rides slowly into the distance, a melancholy journey into nothing. In his place, a pseudo-housewife takes over the screen, pimping for a new, improved, stronger than strong cleaner.

The young man on the sofa stirred his long legs, stretching them lazily out before him. In the seemingly casual and unrehearsed action was a veritable universe of purpose, carefully planned, expertly executed. The muscles of the legs were tensed, swollen to their best advantage. The hips, to all appearances resting lightly upon the sofa, were in fact, thrust upward at a precise angle, the stomach held deliberately flat, the bulge of the genitals displayed in their most effective and enticing—he hoped—position, the chest athletically expanded. Like a skilled and artistic arrangement of flowers, the various and combined charms of this attractive young man were put on show, posed and poised, merchandise intended to attract—and to sell.

"I love this one," he said aloud, turning to the man beside him on the sofa. "I think it's my favorite one of all."

THE *WHY NOT*, by Victor J. Banis

Lee Denver smiled superficially, remembering that the same young man had said the same thing about the last movie they had watched together—or was it the same young man? Where the hell had he met this one, at the *Why Not*? He left the question unanswered, not important enough for real deliberation, and thought again of the movie on television. I'm too young, Lee told himself behind the smiling mask. Too young for my movies to be showing on Saturday afternoon television. Like I'm a Tom Mix, or Hopalong Cassidy, a cowboy relic of some bygone age.

"It had some message," he agreed to the young man's statement without enthusiasm, "I think I was more at home in this role than I was in some of the others."

Involved though he is in his own self-pitying thoughts, he is not unaware of the pose assumed by the man beside him, nor of the wealth of loveliness being offered to him. Nor, although this scene, in infinite variations, has been enacted countless times before, with countless young men, is he really hardened to the thrill, or at least the pride, of being courted, as it were, by the never-ending stream of young men—lovely, charming, studied, some of them quite exciting—who see, in pleasing this aging but still important star, a golden opportunity to springboard their own success.

Aging? I'm not so aging, he thinks, stealing a covert glance at the length of his own body. But the truth is, he is aging. His robe has fallen open and his legs, in contrast to the ones near him, are thin, his knees bony and prominent. His stomach, try though he might to hold it in, no longer obeys his commands without engineering assistance.

Remembering what is expected of him, and compassionately aware of the pains to which this young man has gone to make himself desirable, Lee smiled again at his companion and assumed a mildly flirtatious manner. With one hand he stroked the virile surface of a thigh.

"Wouldn't you be more comfortable without all those clothes on?" he asked. He hoped that this one would be coy, perhaps even refuse for a time to accommodate these advances. It was always a little more interesting when they offered some resistance.

But this one was not coy, not quite skilled enough in this, his secondary trade, to make a game out of the inevitable. He grinned, too obviously pleased with his success, and stood.

"Sure," he replied, beginning without hesitation to strip. His smooth, too-evenly tanned flesh gleamed in the light reflected from the television screen, muscles rippling and dancing as he moved, bent, turned.

The housewife and her cleaner were gone and Lee was uncomfortably aware of the face—his face and yet not quite his face—smiling out at them, like a Peeping Tom, watching the drama being enacted on this side of the screen.

"Jackie says I have a swinging body," the young man comments. "You know, Jackie from the *Why Not*. I'll bet I could have that if I wanted. I'll bet I am the only guy in the place who could make Jackie."

Lee suppresses a smile, wondering if the young man can really believe that he is masculine enough to appeal to Jackie from the *Why Not*, whom he remembers clearly.

Wanting to be polite and yet without genuine interest, Lee tried to watch the strip tease before him, and found himself annoyed when the young stallion, now naked, stepped over his legs, placing himself directly in front of the screen. His flesh swung indolently, a sacrificial offering on the altar of prostitution. Dutifully, Lee leaned forward.

"We'll ride due west," a voice, Lee's voice, said from somewhere beyond the firm, taut buttocks. Lee choked, unnecessarily, and pulled his head away. With a kindly but firm hand he pulled the young man toward him. For a moment there was a trace of hesitation, of resistance, and Lee's hopes soared. But his young lover relented, determined to satisfy, and he kneeled meekly, suddenly less masculine and too submissive.

"I have never known what love is," said Lee, the cowboy, from the television screen. Lee's eyes are riveted now to the screen, watching the handsome man there move about, pose, smile sadly into the reporting cameras. He is only vaguely aware of the wet, warm mouth on his body, trying inexpertly to arouse some passion from the disinterested flesh.

* * * * * * *

Wayne squinted his eyes against the glare of the late afternoon sun and walked as quickly as the shifting sand would allow, a little out of breath from the distance and too much smoking.

One more hill of sand to cross, one more mountain to conquer, and the world of barbecue pits and children playing with empty beer cans would be behind him. Only a few more feet, hurrying against the dragging weight of the sand, over the hill, and he was there, his eyes scanning the beach before him, calculating with electronic precision the number of bodies lying on the beach. Not many today, but then it is off-season, late in the day, and it is rather cool for the beach; especially cool for a bare-ass beach.

Walking slower now, he made his way down the hill of sand, seemingly nonchalant, studying in quick glances the naked bodies stretched out at his feet. It was like walking through a battlefield strewn with the dead. Only, here, the dead examine him too, some of them pleased, some of them not so kind in their judgment, all watching with varying degrees of curiosity to see where he will settle.

He saw nothing of great interest. There was one kid who was attractive, half hard and smiling a carnivorous welcome, but he was not more than sixteen surely. Like seeing himself a few years ago, Wayne thought. Too many years ago, he decided, and went on without a pause. In the distance, all but lost in the hills that sloped upward toward the highway, four feet wriggle and squirm together: someone is being screwed.

Wayne went on, still looking, like a cautious and experienced housewife making her way past the produce counter at the market, shopping for just the right head of lettuce, the perfect tomato. Time was when he would have been followed eagerly down the beach by these worshipers of the sun. Time was when he had been sixteen, too pretty to be believed. But he was thirty now, or near it, striving with fer-

42

vor but without success to look younger, and youth, the never failing aphrodisiac, was abandoning him. Now he had to walk, examine, watch for a telltale sign of interest.

He passed by familiar faces, faces he had seen at the *Why Not* on many a night, but there is a protocol to be observed here: there is no recognition, no friendly greeting, only the silent, withering scrutiny.

He was almost to the end of the beach, and ready to resign himself to a wasted trip, when he saw one man alone on the grassy slope of a hillock. Not so young himself, old enough, in fact, to regard Wayne as young. But handsome still, dignified, fatherly—and smiling hesitantly at Wayne. Wayne returned the smile, veered to the left and approached the smiling stranger. Along the beach, the watching eyes took note, smiled or frowned, and looked elsewhere.

No need for words, but the play must be done, the rules adhered to. Wayne spread his towel on the sand, peeled his bathing suit from his body with the practiced finesse of a stripper, and lowered himself gracefully to the cloth, lying on his back. Counting to himself: one, two, three, four…soon, now…five, six, seven…. He heard the familiar clearing of the throat, inviting attention, and when he turned his head the man was smiling at him, more warmly than before. He was holding himself, his hand moving only slightly.

Wayne hesitated for just the right length of time. Then, eyes, nearly closed, he rolled over, crouching. Nothing said, no need for conversation in this all-too-familiar ritual. The act will form the words for them.

He lost himself in the sensual thrill of contact, the sun warm on his bare back, the sand coarse and clinging to his feet. A hand reached down, gently stroked his shoulder, lazily grateful for the attention.

"I love you," a voice whispered above him.

As though the voice had turned some hidden, sensitive switch, Wayne felt his own body stiffen, shuddering as a weird, magnificent climax swept through him. He crushed his body against the towel.

Then, as though fleeing the demons of hell, he jumped up, hurriedly pulling his suit on again. Dragging his towel behind him, he hurried away, leaving an astonished face behind him and a still unsatisfied need to be dealt with by some other shopper.

To Wayne, it was unimportant, a no longer needed means to an end that had been reached already.

The game, for the afternoon at least, was ended.

THE *WHY NOT*, by Victor J. Banis

4:39 PM

Saturday Afternoon

◄Chapter Two►

"Slowly add one cup of milk...." Ralph read the instructions carefully from the open cookbook and poured the milk, stooping down to be certain that the measure was one cup exactly.

While his attention was focused conscientiously on the cake batter he was stirring, another part of his mind reviewed his wardrobe, selecting and rejecting various outfits for the evening. The black slacks looked the best on him. They were tight, but not ludicrously so, good for his slender hips. Skinny hips, he corrected himself ruefully.

Which was beside the point, because the black slacks would not do at all. The seat was shiny, nearly worn through and there was an ugly stain on one leg that the cleaners had not been able to get out. That left the brown pair, with the baggy seat. He had been heavier when he bought them and they had been taken in twice already. They would have to go to the tailor's again, no doubt, unless he could find some way to gain some weight, a feat he had been trying to accomplish for nearly three years. There was the gray suit, but a suit was hardly the thing for the *Why Not*—and the blue wash pants. Not particularly glamorous, but the blue wash pants were probably the best of the lot.

He finished the cake batter, wondered if the oven had been on long enough to reach the indicated

47

THE *WHY NOT*, by Victor J. Banis

temperature and decided to give it another moment or so while he smoked a cigarette. Soon, like it or not, he would have to shop for some clothing. Not that he wouldn't like some new things. He loved clothes, good things and stylish. But a new suit meant trimming down their budget for at least three months, a budget already pared to an almost minimum. They could have hot dogs, maybe, but Joe didn't like hot dogs. They had hamburger at least twice a week as it was, but maybe he could find a new recipe, some as-yet-untried variation on ground beef.

If I stopped smoking, he thought, without much conviction. That would be a pretty large saving, but it seemed like one ought to be allowed some vices. What else? He was already neurotically careful about keepings lights out to save electricity. They didn't pay the water, so that was no answer. They could, of course, let the savings account go, but that almost certainly meant foregoing next summer's vacation. At any rate, the savings account would suffer enough when tax time came.

How do housewives manage, he wondered, thinking that, of all the feminine traits he had acquired in the course of his young life, household management was not one of them. The married couples he knew, the straight ones, seemed to get along so well on much less money than he and Joe. He didn't make much stocking the shelves at the supermarket, but Joe's salary was a good one, after all: twelve thousand plus a year. That should be enough for all sorts of luxuries. If only there weren't all those bills; but then, if there weren't bills there wouldn't be a delicious new sofa in the living room,

48

or the new drapes—they had been an extravagance, but exactly what they both wanted.

He remembered, finally, the oven, and poured his cake batter quickly into the waiting pans, and slid them hurriedly into the oven.

"How about a drink?" Joe called from the den. Ralph lifted a bottle from the stand near the sink, estimating the quantity of vodka left in it. Enough for two, maybe three drinks. Of course, they would be drinking later at the *Why Not*. Maybe I shouldn't have one now, he thought, turning the question over in his mind. He was not, had never been, a very good drinker, a fact which never failed to cause him embarrassment when they went to parties or, even rarer, bars. He glanced at the stove, calculating the time for the pot roast, and finally mixed two martinis, trying to be sparing on the vodka. What was it Jackie had told him about stretching out liquor? Something he couldn't recall at the moment. He carried the drinks to the den, annoyed to see that, as usual, he was spilling them on the way. His hands, or his sense of balance, or both, were too unsteady.

Joe glanced up, nodding his thanks, and sipped his martini experimentally. He scowled, creasing his pleasantly handsome face, and Ralph knew that he had been too sparing with the vodka, too generous with the vermouth. To his annoyance, Joe uncurled himself from the sofa, laying his book aside to walk into the kitchen. He came back with the bottle, poured another trickle of vodka into his glass, and returned the liquor to the kitchen before settling himself once more with his book.

THE *WHY NOT*, by Victor J. Banis

"You look tired," he commented, glancing over the top of his book at Ralph, and Ralph felt suddenly ashamed at having been annoyed a moment before.

"Just thinking about tonight," he answered, smiling wearily. "I wish I had said no. But Agatha has called so many times...." He let his voice trail away, leaving the sentence, like so many others, unfinished.

"Oh, it will do us both good to get out for a change," Joe assured him, returning his gaze to the book. Ralph tried his own drink, decided that it really wasn't dry enough, and stubbornly refused to doctor it up with more vodka as Joe had done.

Out for a change.... He was not, in truth, looking forward to the evening. There had been other such evenings in the past, most of them in the first year that he and Joe had been together. He remembered several of them, unpleasant occasions when they had quarreled, sometimes violently, over some supposed flirtation, or a conspicuous measure of attention one or the other of them was receiving from someone at the bar.

The quarrels had been frequent then, both of them too possessive, too jealous for any degree of security. But that was largely in the past now; not that they had grown stronger as individuals, but they had grown careful, given up that sort of social life, and mostly they avoided situations charged with temptations or dangers. It was a good life, he thought. They were happy, presumably, with one another.

Ralph stole a quick glance at his lover, totally absorbed now in the novel he was reading. Sexy

THE *WHY NOT*, by Victor J. Banis

Joe, the catch of the season. I'm not pretty, Ralph thought with some wonderment—too effeminate, too thin, rather awkward with people—a worrier and an absolute genius for saying and doing the wrong thing. It seemed like he had spent half his life with his foot in his mouth. How did I get him, he asked himself, an often-asked question. So many others with their eyes on him, so many that he would seem to have preferred. But here I am, going on three years and looking like a long time more.

He jumped, remembering suddenly that he had forgotten to time the cake. Annoyed with himself, he glanced at his watch, trying to calculate how long it had been in the oven already. In his annoyance, he clumsily spilled his drink again, this time on his lap. He squealed with frustration.

Joe shot him an annoyed glance over the top of his book. "What's the matter with you today?" he asked, not so much concerned as angry that his chain of thought had been broken.

It's very difficult, Ralph wanted to say, trying to build a different kind of life. I'm not the perfect little housekeeper you think I am, you know. I'm not really a good cook, and my budget, the one you are so proud of, and boast of to our friends, doesn't work at all. And I am not at all strong, or practical, the way you think, or clever...

"I'm just not with it today, I guess," he said instead, rubbing his hand over the damp spot in his lap. Suddenly gentle again, in some way moved by the pathetic little face, Joe leaned over, ran a hand affectionately through the straw like hair.

THE *WHY NOT*, by Victor J. Banis

"You need to relax more. You work too hard around the house," he said sincerely, his eyes soft and soothing with their tenderness.

Ralph leaned toward the comforting arms, starting to relax and then, with a grimace, sniffed the air. "Damn," he snapped, jumping to his feet. "The cake is burning."

* * * * * * *

The afternoon still too long. Try to pass the time, feeling not too well at all—a cold, maybe? Or, more likely a hangover from the night before. Try the steam baths, a well-trained voice within tells me, and out I set for the baths, not so much caring for them as needing a purpose, a movement toward some destination.

Ignore the leering smile of the man at the counter who checks my valuables and wonders if he can arrange to follow me inside briefly, to take advantage of my obvious search, maybe to find what he himself is searching for.

The walls inside are rotting and musty, the floor dirty and unswept. Only a single customer in the locker area, a fat old man, eyeing me with interest but without hope as I strip. Cruelly I pose to heighten his appreciation, give him plenty to admire, and time to admire it, coolly aloof and impervious to his desire.

Upstairs, the darkened chamber reserved for sexual encounters is a snake pit of arms and legs, bodies writhing and twisting together, the smell of sperm overpowering and alarming. Someone follows me in, an arm slipping about my waist, but it is the old man from the locker room, made bolder now in the darkness and the universality of the chamber's activities.

I shrug off his arm, and leave the room. Retreating back down the stairs, to the steam room, where the sperm smell is still strong and supplemented by another less pleasant odor. The heat, as one climbs higher on the benches, grows devastating, until one ceases to care when a body approaches, the unseen face of a stranger seeks my flesh and I am caught up in the act of fulfillment, weakly and mechanically performing until I shudder and draw away. The body goes, but not before another approaches, standing above me.

The door opens, a shaft of light in the darkness, and the room becomes for an instant a frozen tableau, everyone motionless, wary. But the newcomer is too young to be Tillie Law, young and pretty—too pretty, I tell myself, a lovely flower to be thrown into the muck and mire before him. In the fleeting light, the jackals can be seen crouching, tensely poised for the attack. The door closes and the movement begins, vultures moving in upon the newcomer, vying for positions. A new conquest, fresh meat upon which to feed.

Finally, wearied with the parade, unending and infinitely varied in its sameness, of bodies— large bodies, small bodies, short and long bodies, fat and thin bodies—I leave the steam room, make my way down the corridor, blinking my eyes against the glare of the harsh naked lights.

Here, in one of the small rooms, inadequately partitioned from one another, I find an empty cot and throw myself upon it, not sleeping but not quite awake either.

Soon, all too soon, someone enters. I half open my eyes to see him, the man reclining on the other cot. Handsome, masculine—too handsome, perhaps, too masculine. Twenty-nine, maybe thirty, desirable and aware of his beauty—altogether too dangerous. Too likely to be vice, and I resist the silent, screaming voice within me, remain limp and unmoving until I feel the seeking hand stretching across the space between us to clasp my fingers. I turn, fighting within myself a whirlwind of feelings, watch him with dull eyes as he comes to me, sits beside me. He embraces me all at once, a desperate, fervent embrace and then, with a suddenness that is too great to comprehend, he stands again and he is gone. No kiss, no groping, sucking, moaning. A wild, terrified embrace before dashing off to battle.

Maybe, after all, he was vice. With a problem of his own. That happened, too. There was generally a reason, after all, for a man to choose that line of work. What gratification would a normal man, a real man, get out of cruising other men in a bathhouse? What man could bear it, without the incentive of pleasure? Even I can hardly bear it.

Unable to suffer myself longer, I leave and make my way back to the locker room. I avoid the mirror there, expecting to find that my flesh is gone, ripped from me by the frantic clawing of teeth and mouths, but the mirror defeats me, remains stubbornly in my way, and I see myself, whole after all, a ghost of reflection in the glass—the reflection more real, perhaps, than I myself.

THE *WHY NOT*, by Victor J. Banis

* * * * * * *

Lon knew, from the first ring of the phone, that it would be Jackie. He knew too, long before the preliminary conversation was ended and the real purpose of the call broached, what the news was going to be.

"Sweetheart, I can't make it after all tonight," Jackie managed to say finally.

"Who's surprised?" Lon said dryly.

"Now don't be that way." A pause for some comment, which was not forthcoming. "Lindy is all alone at the bar tonight. He's got nobody else available. I couldn't just leave him in the lurch, don't you see?"

"You will have to one of these days, won't you?"

"I know, but not tonight. Tell me you still love me."

Lon sighed. That was a customary diversion, and usually a successful one. "Madly," he declared without enthusiasm. "But I would much rather love you on a more reasonable time schedule."

"I can see you later. We can have the whole night together. I won't let you go to sleep until dawn." Jackie's voice was teasing, attempting to soothe over the ruffled spirits.

It was pointless arguing, Lon knew. The decisions had already been made. His approval or disapproval would not really change anything.

"Until dawn?" he asked, relenting.

"At the earliest." Jackie's relief was evident. "Will you pick me up?"

"I'd rather not."

Oh, really, you are being the stubborn one to-day. You know I hate running around town by my-self late at night, and I can hardly ask Lindy to drop me off."

"I don't like the people that come to your bar, if you want to argue the point," Lon said. "They're too faggoty for my taste."

"I go there."

"You're different."

Jackie giggled. "That's the nicest thing any-one has said to me all day."

"Damn it!" Lon swore without thinking. "Why do you have to make a joke of everything? Can't you ever be serious?"

"I will be tonight, until dawn, I promise. Come by about one?"

"Catch a cab."

"I'm broke."

"Lindy didn't give you any money this week?"

"He hadn't been to the bank yet. And I spent the last of my money at the doctor's."

'What doctor's?" Lon was quick to pounce on that. "Are you sick?"

The pause this time was a lengthy one. Jackie laughed finally. "I don't know why you make such a fuss about everything. Maybe I'm going to have my sex changed. They can do that now, you know. I think they can, anyway."

"Like hell you will!"

"Spoken like the man I love. See you at one?"

The battle, Lon decided, was over, and as usual, not in his favor. "See you at one."

THE *WHY NOT*, by Victor J. Banis

* * * * * * *

Grace Winston cocked her head and listened for the sound of footsteps on the stairs. On the chair opposite her, her sister, Agnes, continued her incessant chatter.

Why doesn't she stop talking for just one minute? Grace thought bitterly, and then, feeling slightly guilty at having thought so unfair a thought, she smiled and tried again to concentrate on her sister's endless conversation.

"I must say, you seem edgy these days," Agnes said aloud, studying her sister's face carefully. 'You are taking care of yourself, aren't you?"

Grace, embarrassed at having been caught at what was nothing more than inattention, blushed and bobbed her head emphatically. "Oh, I'm fine, really. I just had something on my mind."

Agnes snorted disdainfully and took another sip of her coffee. "You're like a chicken on a hot tin roof," she said. "And, you've lost some weight, I notice."

"Well, it isn't as though I can't afford to lose a few pounds," Grace replied, laughing slightly as she patted one plump hip. "But I *am* fine. I guess I'm just tired from cleaning."

"That is no wonder. I have never understood how a woman could work and keep up a house, too. Don't snap at me the way you usually do, but I still think you should be married."

"Oh, no," Grace shook her head emphatically. "I have no desire for another man. It took me too long and too much trouble to get rid of the last one." This, delivered with a smile, was nonetheless tinged

57

with a certain bitterness, a bitterness that was, after all, very nearly the only thing she had ever gotten from her divorced husband.

"Oh, for Pete's sake, that's been twelve years. If you'd have taken my advice, you would have married the day the divorce was final. And I know that school teacher, what was his name...?"

"Dennis," Grace said. An image of dear, bookish Dennis, boring Dennis, popped into her mind.

"Yes, that one, I know he was interested. Mark was just a child then, and I think a boy needs a father."

Yes, I suppose they do, Grace thought silently, cocking her head again. Not that she had not tried, in every way, to make up for the lack. She *had* been a good mother to Mark. She had worked hard to see him through school, and now through college. But then, probably a boy did need a father, although it seemed to her that none at all would be preferable to the one he had had.

"Excuse me for a moment," she said abruptly, standing. "Help yourself to more coffee. I want to see Mark for a moment."

She left Agnes in the living room and made her way upstairs, pausing outside Mark's door with some timidity. She knew that he did not like to be bothered when his door was closed. Finally, realizing that he would have heard her come up the stairs anyway, would wonder why she was lingering outside, she knocked lightly at the door. He opened it a moment later and he was, she could see at a glance, annoyed.

58

THE *WHY NOT*, by Victor J. Banis

"Are you going out again?" she asked, pretending to be oblivious to his annoyance. When he stepped back, she came on into the room. It was a nice room, a little old-womanish, perhaps, but then Mark was rather a delicate and conservative young man and the room seemed, somehow, to fit him.

"Just for a while," he told her, returning his attention to the mirror and the act of combing his hair. "I won't be late."

It's late already, she thought, but did not say it aloud. "Will you be bringing a friend home?" It seemed to her that he started slightly at the question, but he recovered quickly and resumed his efforts with his not very manageable hair.

"Yes, I think so," he answered after a rather embarrassing silence. "Unless you would rather I didn't?"

"Oh, I don't mind," she assured him quickly. "You have such nice friends. I liked the one who came last weekend especially. Although...." She hesitated before going on. "...Sometimes I think they don't care much for me."

He frowned, gave his hair a final pat, and placed the comb precisely on the surface of the dresser. "What an odd thing to say," he said. "What would make you think that?"

"Oh, I don't know," she forced a laugh, not a very natural-sounding one. "They never come back again. They must think I'm an ogre."

"Don't be silly," he told her, selecting a sweater from the dresser. From the way that he said it, she knew there would not be any further explanation. She walked over to him, meekly, and picked an imaginary piece of lint from the shoulder of the sweater. Their eyes met, for an instant, in the mirror, and she was painfully aware of the distance between them, of the rotting, stagnating questions that she wanted to ask and dared not. Instead, she dropped her eyes to the surface of the dresser.

"The *Why Not*." She read the printing on the matchbook cover and chuckled aloud. "What a strange name for a night club."

He grabbed the matches and cigarettes rather brusquely from the dresser, shoving them into his shirt pocket. "Got to go," he told her, giving her a quick peck on the cheek.

She left the room with him, noting with some resentment that he remembered to lock the door. He's entitled to his privacy, isn't he, she reminded herself? In the hall downstairs, he gave her another brief hug, waved goodbye to his Aunt Agnes through the open door to the living room, and he was gone. Grace returned to her place at the sofa and drank a mouthful of her nearly cold coffee.

"How is Mark doing in school?" Agnes asked, beginning to gather her things together, preparatory to leaving. Grace could not help feeling relief.

"Oh, quite well," Grace assured her, deciding that the coffee was too cold to drink. "I think he will be a very fine musician."

"My Frank has to work so hard to keep his grades up," Agnes remarked, snapping her purse closed. "But of course he lives for his sports, and he is quite an athlete. Don't you think it's funny that Mark never takes any interest in sports?"

THE *WHY NOT*, by Victor J. Banis

"Oh, for heaven's sake, Agnes," Grace snapped. "People can't be all alike, you know." But why not, she asked herself silently?

* * * * * * *

Joaquin was always an early comer, and unlike many others who arrived about the same time he did, around nine, he also left early. He was, in fact, in many ways different from the others who frequented the *Why Not*. Where many of them made of the tawdry bar a home away from home, spending the greater part of every evening in its womb-like shelter, Joaquin came only once a week, Friday night or more rarely, as on this occasion, Saturday night. Unlike most of them, who tended to stagnate, becoming increasingly unable to tear themselves away, he was a transient who came, had a drink or perhaps two at the most, and left. In contrast to the variety of sweaters, competitively flamboyant shirts, slacks and jeans that the crowd wore, Joaquin was elegantly dressed, his Negro face in sharp contrast to the stiff whiteness of his shirt, his tie carefully and precisely knotted, the suit always immaculate and stylish.

Joaquin would have been more in place, indeed, in one of the city's finer clubs or restaurants, a handsome, well-bred man about town—or rather, man about several towns, for Joaquin was a traveler. The neat leather suitcase that he carried with him on his visits to the bar was a traditional and expected part of his costume, a trademark that he carried proudly.

THE *WHY NOT*, by Victor J. Banis

This night, as on each of his visits, the regulars and the bartenders greeted Joaquin with a mixture of warm regard and subdued envy—nodding, smiling, some of them laying a friendly hand on his shoulder as he moved briskly past them. Others, of course, were more flirtatious, openly looking him up and down, for Joaquin was rightly looked upon as a real prize, the more so because to the best of their knowledge he never left with anyone, or gave more than polite consideration to any of the numerous propositions that he invariably received in the course of his all-too-brief visits.

"Hey, it's Joaquin," Lindy greeted him from behind the bar. Only once had Lindy made the mistake of greeting his customer as Jock, and the polite but firm reminder that the name was Joaquin had been heard and remembered by all the regulars present, so that now no one would dream of such informality. "Where are you off to this week?"

The question, carried through a large section of the bar by Lindy's habit of speaking loudly, produced the usual amount of attention, for Joaquin was always traveling somewhere, and his travels were of the sort to interest the frequenters of the *Why Not*. Even those who did not know him personally would pause to hear about the business executive who was taking Joaquin to his cabin in the mountains for the weekend, or the movie actress, more often than not an idol of the boys, who had singled Joaquin out for her attentions.

Once it had been a French count, traveling briefly through the country, who had, in return for Joaquin's admirable favors, presented the young man with a diamond-bedecked watch which he always wore now. Sometimes, although not too often, Joaquin's week had been apparently less successful, for he would be embarking on a trip alone, but nonetheless interesting, and the careful listener would hear, on his next visit to the bar, of an exciting weekend spent in San Francisco, or Seattle, or perhaps even New York City.

It was an exciting life that the tall young Negro lived, a source of envy and admiration on the part of the others at the bar, and Joaquin, despite his apparent nonchalance, reveled in their interest. His soft, caressing voice, always low, was pitched just slightly higher so that his listeners need not miss the tantalizing details of his adventures, and although he sat at the bar and seldom turned except to reply to some greeting, his limpid eyes kept a careful watch in the mirror behind the bar, tuned to the delicate moods of his audience until, after a brief time, they would begin to direct their attention elsewhere. This was the time, usually after one drink sipped slowly, that Joaquin would pick up his suitcase from the floor, gulp an ice cube from the glass into his mouth and, with a friendly nod to Lindy, depart for his journey of the week.

This time, however, Joaquin was not quite himself. "It's just a touch of something," he explained to Lindy when his drink, the usual very fine Scotch, on the rocks, a water back, was set in front of him. By the more than casual observer, it might have been seen that Joaquin was just a trifle less neat and well groomed than usual, his tie barely off center, a piece of lint overlooked on his lapel. Certainly there was nothing sloppy about his appearance, only confirmation of the fact that he had "a touch of something" and had not applied quite the usual diligence to making ready.

"So, the Count's back in town," Lindy commented, taking advantage, as he always did, of Joaquin's audience to share the spotlight. Joaquin, it seemed, was playing a return engagement with the Count of the past, this time off to Monterey for a brief but lavish fling with his admirer. "He must have liked what he got," Lindy opined aloud, thinking to himself that he could hardly blame the Count. In truth, he would have liked a sample himself, but having never detected any trace of response in his customer, he had made no attempt to satisfy his desire. Too, there was no telling how Jackie would react...he remembered suddenly that Jackie was not there yet. The bar would be getting busy soon; he would need the help. Too bad, he thought fleetingly, about that night off...probably it was not anything important anyway, though. Most likely it was Lon, making noises.

"Man, you gotta give 'em happies, that's all," Joaquin was saying. He spoke in a dialect that was rather his own, a curious mixture of slang, guttural and odd terminology that had become, over a period of time, an integral part of his charm. "Give me a chance to shove it to them. Hell, even show it to 'em, and I've got 'em won. But this one, he loves it like nobody. He is wantin' me to zoom back to France with him. Says he wants me to meet his Mama."

This, delivered with a grin, was greeted the same way, as a bit of humor not to be accepted as genuine. Joaquin was not the marrying sort, whether or not the Count might be. He might bestow a

weekend on the fortunate admirer, sometimes a re-
peat performance, but no more than that.

The drink went slowly tonight and Joaquin,
feeling only slightly better as a result of it, was not
as sparkling as he might ordinarily have been, although with his "touch of something" he found that
he really did not mind the premature loss of his audience.

And they, the others about him, perhaps disappointed that his conquest for the week was not a
new one but only a repetition, and no doubt conscious too of Joaquin's less-than-customary charm,
had begun, before the drink was half finished, to
move more freely about the room, watch more
closely the entrance of newcomers through the
draped door, and in general to display evidence that
the importance of Joaquin's visit was, for the evening, fading.

This time Joaquin went to the restroom. That
was, had anybody thought about it, a singular event.
On any other night, his time in the bar would have
been spent on his stool, stationary until time for his
departure. But this time he had to go. For a moment
or two he fought against the desire. He did not like
to use public restrooms; restrooms like the one here
where everybody could conveniently see everybody
else and the patrons always took advantage of the
convenience.

"This damned cold," he grumbled to himself.
Like it or not, he was going to have to go. He got up
from the stool slowly, noticed by very few of his re-
cent admirers, and made his way briskly and deliberately to the rear, to the door marked MEN.

THE *WHY NOT*, by Victor J. Banis

At least, he thought with some relief, the place was not crowded yet. A solitary queen, whom he recognized as one called Linda, was just stepping back from the urinal. Joaquin stood aside, necessary in the cramped quarters, to allow the willowy thing to pass and get to the washbasin before stepping himself to the urinal.

At the washbasin, Linda washed his hands with increasing thoroughness, his eyes on the mirror in which he could see without obstruction the scene at the urinal. He looked Joaquin up and down with a hungry eye. His tongue darted out to brush against his lips as he contemplated the rather striking example of masculine endowment being shown. Like most of the others around the bar, Linda had heard the rather outlandish stories and rumors about Joaquin's physical attributes and had, with an affected indifference, pooh-poohed the accounts as too preposterous. But there it was, the sort a fairy's dreams are made of. And it was close enough, he thought as he turned the off the water finally, that he could reach out and touch it. And he did exactly that.

"You must get awfully tired holding that big thing all by yourself," he crooned, grabbing a handful just as Joaquin concluded the business at hand.

The quick and unexpected movement produced a lightning quick change in Joaquin's usually placid behavior. His hand shot out, striking smartly against the cheek of the startled queen.

"Knock it off!" he snarled viciously, his face contorted. And Linda did. Holding a hand to his cheek, he fairly flew from the restroom, back into the crowded safety of the bar, leaving Joaquin trembling and shaken behind him. Joaquin stood for a

66

moment, breathing deeply, trying to restore his calm.

"Easy, baby," he whispered to himself and then, not wanting to be seen so shaken when he returned to the bar, he pulled a cigarette from his pocket, lit it, and inhaled deeply, leaning against the washbasin.

"Dirty bitch," Linda fumed to himself as he swished back along the length of the bar. "Who in the name of Sadie's ass does he think he is, anyway, slapping decent people around?" For a moment he considered making a scene out of the incident, but the fear that Joaquin might become even more dangerous prompted him to discard that idea. Instead, he decided to have another drink. He pushed his way up to the bar, cursing when his foot struck something that almost tripped him. He looked down angrily and saw Joaquin's suitcase, sitting where he had left it next to his stool.

Beaming with malicious merriment, he glanced quickly around. No one was paying him any attention. Here, he assured himself, was a chance for quick revenge. He could toss a lighted cigarette into the case and burn that bastard's pretty wardrobe to ashes. Or maybe, he thought, there would be a chance to humiliate Joaquin with its contents. Wouldn't everybody just crap if that damned thing were packed full of drag, or something equally fruity?

Holding his breath, he ducked down and flicked the latch of the case. It wasn't locked, a fact which he owed, without knowing it, to Joaquin's cold and the resultant negligence. Two quick movements and the case was open, its contents exposed to his astonished eyes.

Forgetting discretion, or rather abandoning it, Linda let out a veritable shriek of delight. "Mary," he screamed to no one and everyone. "You girls are not going to believe this!"

Joaquin emerged a moment later from the restroom to be greeted by a burst of laughter, the sort of laughter that included the entire crowd, now pushed together around his stool. He realized, with a start, that they were all turning their heads merrily in his direction, watching with a mysterious glee as he made his way back to his stool and his drink. Not until he had shouldered his way through the giggling throng, however, and reached its relative center, did he see the open suitcase. His heart seemed to stop beating, and for a second he wanted to lash out, strike somebody, even kill. The anger fled, to be replaced by a burning shame that swept through him, paling his dark skin.

"You and the Count planning on reading a lot?" somebody called, and that touched off a fresh burst of laughter. Without answering, Joaquin knelt and began to gather up the bundles of wadded newspaper, stuffing them forlornly back into the suitcase from which they had been emptied. Paper—crumpled, torn newspaper. "I should have packed some clothes this time," he thought painfully, fighting back the tears that were welling up in his eyes. "Fucking bastards, how did they get it open?"

The laughter about him was generously seasoned with derisive comments. "Weekend trips!

THE *WHY NOT*, by Victor J. Banis

Fucking phony! Who did she think she was fooling with those silly stories of hers?"

The suitcase repacked and shut, Joaquin stood. For a brief second his eyes met Lindy's and, despite the grin, he saw in the bartender's eyes a touch of something that might have been—what? Sympathy? Pity? And which, somehow, seemed even worse than the gibes from the rest of the bar.

In the mirror behind Lindy, he saw the howling faces, mocking and jeering. Head down, he turned and made his way through the crowd, oblivious to the comments, to the hands which now boldly groped and patted him, ripping away the shreds of dignity and respect that he had worn so proudly. He reached the door, finally, after an eternity of struggling, and left the *Why Not*, never to return.

* * * * * * *

Night at last, still early enough to make the rounds before hurrying away to the Why Not, to the domain of Lindy and Jackie. Time enough for another dim little room where the young men cluster about a player piano, singing or just yelling at the tops of their voices. Their mouths opened wide, eyes lifting upward, looking like so many hungry little birds begging to be fed, hungry for the all-essential worm that soothes. "Give my regards to Broadway...." and for a chorus or so there is something between them, holding them all together, a camaraderie, almost.

Lost, lonely souls joined together in their private, pregnant hell. But a new face joins the group, a young, pretty face, and the camaraderie is gone in

69

an instant, replaced by familiar tensions, the singing automatic and hollow now as the singers listen for another music. In the corner, protected by the singers from general sight, a queen crouches on her knees, does homage to that most fickle of all subjects. Thick-glassed steins of beer lift high. Pretty-face has found a singing partner for his duet of love. Another prize is won, and lost, and the chorus begins again, voices loud, hips swaying. "Give my regards to Broadway...."

Drifting on to still another meeting place, or is it the same? Darkness, swaying bodies, furtive hands, haunting smiles, the inevitable mirror. But the singing is on the stage, where a fat boy wearing a wide, billowing skirt over his slacks—not actual drag, then, and so not a cause for arrest—mouths the words to a show tune, the real music blaring from a phonograph backstage.

Here there are tourists as well, young couples out to see "the world." A wife laughs too loudly, clings too zealously to her husband, who returns the smiles of the boys with too much kindness. He would like to go with one of them, try his luck at the game, but she talks still louder, incessantly, demanding his dutiful attention, and when he looks up again the young man he was watching has left, spirited away by some less timid seeker.

The chorus of angels laughs with, or at, the antics of the fat boy, and his partners join him now in a rousing number, punctuated by winks and smiles at the audience. For a moment, the stage is dark, the audience taking advantage of the pause to reexamine the room and the crowd. The lights come up again and this time the voice is a familiar one, a

70

little girl's voice seeking to find, over a distant rainbow of tears, a better place. Another boy, ludicrous almost in a poignantly touching manner, kneels in a spotlight of blue, mouths the words precisely. The room is hushed now, each intent face singing silently along, self-pitying, serious, far away until the song has ended and the room explodes with applause that is not so much for the performer as for one's self.

Time is passing now, trickling down the throat with the inevitable drinks. Time enough for one brief stop, a traditional stop at another bar, where a movie is in progress, a trivial, not-so-amusing cartoon that gives its viewers an excuse to laugh at themselves. Here rugged, sullen men pose studiously, well aware of their loveliness, less interested in communication than in appreciation. The wax museum, its detractors call it, a chamber of horrors that will sooner or later draw all unto itself, death a form of life, beauty an ugly end to be achieved at any cost.

At the tables some are eating, but it is not their leathery steaks that they take into their mouths—rather, it is the hard and hardened bodies that drift by their tables, skin-tight clothing, sharply outlined genitals. A dance is in progress, awesome, terrifying, strangely captivating...one, two, three, pose, turn, promenade, one, two, three...unending, whirling away into infinity, sweeping the night before.

Time now for the Why Not, time for the greatest of all shows, the Queen of Queens. Around the world tonight, tomorrow may be too late....

THE *WHY NOT*, by Victor J. Banis

* * * * * * *

Vince glanced up as he parked his car. The window of Norman's apartment appeared dark. The experienced observer, however, would note the almost imperceptible glow and realize that beyond the concealing blinds and the heavy velvet draperies, flickering candles were burning.

"Little old lady from Pasadena," they called Norman, and it was not only the fact that he lived in Pasadena that made the description appropriate. Everything about Norman, from his willowy appearance to his manner of living, suggested some belle dame of a bygone age. In his apartment he was surrounded by the needlepoint he himself had done, by dim lights and roaring fireplaces. Rare old wines lent their dark-hued glamour to the gilt and crystal glassware; the lace cloth over the table would be covered now with old, exquisitely beautiful china and silver, as they always were when Norman entertained.

As he mounted the stairs to the second-floor apartment, no elevator here, Vince imagined what the evening would be—they were usually much the same. Once a month, perhaps once in two months, Norman would call, or send little notes, inviting a handful of people for dinner. They were, most often, the same handful. Vince was the newcomer, for he had known Norman only slightly over a year, while the others had been lifelong friends. Vince was the youngster, too, despite the fact that he was thirty.

There would be cocktails and rather uninteresting conversation, followed by a good, although not inspired dinner, and then coffee and liqueurs. By eleven they would depart, not to see one another until the next quiet little dinner.

Vince had wondered, from time to time, what they did, those low-voiced, aging queens with whom he gathered in Norman's apartment. How did they occupy themselves between dinners, what were their amusements? Despite the several meetings, with no lack of talk, he knew little about them. For that matter, he knew little enough about Norman, beyond that he was fussy, neat, very gentle and thoughtful.

Norman answered the knock at the door promptly, giving Vince's hand a welcoming squeeze and leaning forward to peck Vince's cheek. He wore, as usual, a faded lavender scent that was unpleasant and yet at the same time rather comfortably so, a familiar annoyance that was not, after all, objectionable.

For the most part Vince had been right in his forecast of the evening. Henry and Ron were here, Norman's oldest friends, and a couple of many years standing. Helena, whose real, masculine name Vince did not remember if he had ever heard it. Helena was just Helena. Leroy and Frank and Ernest, who made wigs for a living.

This time, however, there was a stranger. Unlike the others, who waved, or smiled their greetings, this one had risen and was waiting a bit nervously to shake hands.

It would be difficult, Vince found himself thinking, to imagine anyone more out of place. "This is Dean," Norman was saying, and Vince's hand was clasped and squeezed almost painfully.

THE *WHY NOT*, by Victor J. Banis

Dean could not have been more than eighteen, handsome in a crude, awkward way. He walked with legs bowed, suggesting a Western-out-of-doors setting, and his voice, too was noticeably Western—Oklahoma, Vince concluded as Dean remarked how pleased he was to meet him.

It was not only his age, nor the fact that he was so blatantly, almost embarrassingly masculine that made Dean so out of place. Nor was it the fact that he was plainly feeling his drinks—Norman's martinis were quite potent—and, in contrast to the polished, gracious manners about the room, he was clumsy and awkward.

Most startling of all, most conspicuous in the tidiness of Norman's little parlor—filled by neatly dressed aging men whose fingers glittered with diamonds and whose trousers spoke of fine tailoring—was the fact that Dean was badly dressed. And dirty. His faded shirt was actually torn at the pocket and he wore jeans—not even clean jeans, but dirty ones that might have been worn for weeks without washing. His face was washed and shaved, true, but his hands looked grimy and his nails might have been in mourning, as Colette would have put it—they were black.

"Who is he anyway?" Vince asked Helena when he got the chance. "Surely not a visiting cousin from the country?"

Helena chuckled in his usual refined manner. "Hardly, my dear. That's Norman's latest. Minerva alone knows where he found it."

"Norman's latest?" Vince could scarcely believe he had heard correctly. "You must be joking. Why, he's dirty, a crude, boorish hick."

74

THE *WHY NOT*, by Victor J. Banis

Helena gave him an amused glance. "Heavens, you mean you've never seen any of them before? They are all like this, all of Norman's little playmates. He seems to find disgusting synonymous with masculine. But it is his business, I say, and I have to admit some of them are handsome. If this one had a bath, he would be sort of nice, actually, wouldn't he?"

Leroy, who had moved closer to listen to the conversation, waved his hand in dismissal. "Pooh, who needs a bath? One slide and they're clean, that's what I say."

"Ugh, you're vulgar," Helena told him with a grimace.

Vince was trying to digest the bit of gossip. Norman, so prissy, so proper—who would have suspected that his taste ran to this type, so diametrically opposite? And, as though determined to exaggerate the differences, Norman was providing his young friend with yet another drink. Dean would not be able to walk to the table, Vince was certain.

Dinner was later than usual and, as Vince had suspected, it proved necessary to help Dean to reach the table. The husky young cowboy, for he was from Oklahoma, staggered and weaved as Henry and Ron steered him to the table and managed, not without some difficulty, to get him seated.

Vince was vaguely displeased as he found himself assigned to the neighboring chair. He did not like the situation, nor did he particularly like the young man beside him, although in some peculiar way he felt vaguely sorry for him.

His discomfort increased as he became aware of an unexpected and unpleasant scent: body odor, emanating from Dean's direction. From the aroma, it must have been days since the youth had bathed. Vince gritted his teeth in annoyance.

"This is some place," Dean said, speaking directly to Vince and slurring his words.

"Have you been in town long?" Vince asked to be polite.

"Just a couple of days," Dean said. "I hitchhiked here from Oklahoma. Couldn't find a job there, so I came here. Say, you don't like me, do you?"

Vince started and blushed. He had not realized his distaste was so obvious. "I can't say I like or dislike you," he answered, not wanting to hurt the young man. "I hardly know you."

"I know what you are," Dean told him with what was apparently intended for a conspiratorial grin and wink.

Vince raised one eyebrow. "Do you, now?"

Dean leaned closer, his breath unpleasant. His hand rested heavily on Vince's knee. "You're one of those queers, ain't you? They call them gay here, but we call them queers back in Oklahoma."

"What did Norman tell you about this evening?" Vince asked in a low voice.

Dean shrugged, swaying dangerously in his chair. "Just said he was having a few friends in, that's all. Would I like to come up and say hello."

Vince understood then. The boy wasn't gay, not even understanding. He was only stupid, and drunk. Totally blind drunk by the time the meal was ended. Henry helped Norman get him into the bedroom and Vince took advantage of the opportunity to find his coat.

76

THE *WHY NOT*, by Victor J. Banis

"Stick around," Helena told him, seeing him slip into his coat. "Norman says we'll all have a little fun with this one."

"Sorry," Vince told him, a little more curtly than was necessary. "I have a date for later this evening." It was not quite the truth; he had only halfway agreed to meet his friend, Mike, at the *Why Not*; but he did not care to linger to see what the others had in store for the young cowboy.

"Hey, you want to see something enormous?" Henry asked, poking his head around the corner from the bedroom.

"Won't he be sore," Ernest asked, although he moved quickly toward the bedroom.

"He's passed out cold," Henry was explaining as Vince let himself out the front door. "Honey, we could do anything we wanted with him and he would never know. He won't even remember, either."

* * * * * * *

Mike Tanner saw, almost without being aware of it, the figure at the side of the road, thumb extended, and was half stopped before he really gave any conscious thought to what he was doing. A hitchhiker, young looking. More often than not they could be had. Young stuff, that was always nice. Still, he was late already, supposed to meet the crowd at the *Why Not*.

I'll just see what he looks like, he decided, waiting for the running figure to reach the car. If he's okay, I'll give it a whirl. If he's not, I can always drop him in a couple of lights and go on.

THE *WHY NOT*, by Victor J. Banis

The door opened and a young boy slid quickly into the seat beside him. Mike sized him up in one sweeping glance. Sixteen, maybe seventeen, redhead, trim, exciting young body, nice smile. The kid was breathing heavily from the sprint to the car.

"How far you going?" he asked, giving Mike the benefit of that smile again. A friendly little devil, Mike thought, and smiled back.

"Quite a ways," he answered, starting the car up again. This one was nice, well worth a try. He would much rather have a few minutes with something like this than meet those silly queens anyway.

He drove automatically, stealing frequent and not too covert glances in the direction of his rider. "Out on the town tonight?" he asked, a standard opening, a good lead into the real subject.

"No, just over to my girl's house. She's grounded till her grades get better, so we worked on some homework for a while, till her folks said I had better head for home."

Mike gave a well-rehearsed laugh, winking conspiratorially at the smiling youth. "Did you make out before they broke it up?"

The kid laughed, a little self-consciously, and shook his head. "I wish I had. But they didn't leave us alone long enough."

"Too bad," Mike agreed sympathetically. "Hell of a waste of a Saturday night. What do you do, go home and beat the meat?"

The kid laughed again, a slightly nervous laugh, and blushed. "Sometimes," he admitted reluctantly. "But that gets kind of dull."

"Yeah," Mike nodded, encouraged. "You need a buddy. Ever try that sort of thing?"

78

THE *WHY NOT*, by Victor J. Banis

The youth shot him a glance, guarded but not unfriendly. "Yeah, once or twice. You're not the Law, are you?"

Mike's laugh was genuine this time. "No. Don't worry about that. I was just thinking, when I was your age I had a buddy. We used to have some fun together."

His companion relaxed again, deciding apparently that Mike was safe. "Yeah, I got a buddy like that. He stays over at my house a lot and we fool around some."

"Do you like it? Fooling around with him?" Mike asked, his throat a little dry.

"It's pretty good—not like a girl, but if you haven't got a girl around, it's better than nothing."

Mike was definitely encouraged now. "Do you want to fool around some now?" he asked. "With me, I mean?"

It was blunt, and the kid gave him a surprised look. This was the moment of truth, and Mike kept his eyes on the road. He breathed an excited sigh when the kid finally answered, "Sure, why not?"

Mike gave a quick thought to location. They were pretty far from his apartment. It would take a while to drive back there, maybe give the kid time to change his mind.

"Know any place safe around here where we can go?" he asked. It was a gamble, but the chances were that this was not the first time the kid had said yes in the course of hitchhiking, not as quickly as he had agreed, without any coaxing.

He was right. "Yeah," the boy said after a reflective pause. "Take a right at the next traffic light."

THE *WHY NOT*, by Victor J. Banis

Grinning with excitement, Mike turned as directed, started down an ordinary residential street. Ahead of them loomed a large shopping center, the stores and markets closed at this hour.

"Take the alley," the kid instructed, and when they were in the alley, he indicated the back entrance into the vast parking area for the shopping center. They were behind the stores, shielded by them from the bright lights in the front of the mall. It was a good spot for what they had in mind, Mike agreed. The kid obviously had been through this sort of thing before.

He flicked off the lights and coasted to a stop in the center of the parking area. Too far from any apartments or the streets to be seen clearly, enough light that they could see anybody approaching in time to make themselves presentable. He left the motor running for safety and turned to his companion.

Man, this one is hot, he thought happily. The kid had already taken it out of his pants, and was ready and waiting across the seat.

It was pleasant and exciting. The silence was broken only by their breathing and the occasional squeak of the springs. The kid's hands held lightly but firmly to Mike's shoulders, one hand lifting occasionally to stroke Mike's hair. What a sweetheart, Mike thought, really enjoying himself.

It was over too soon, the youth's body growing rigid and lifting off the seat in a brief spasm. Mike held to him, wanting to savor the moment, but the moment the orgasm had ended, the hands on his shoulders pushed him roughly away. Mike lifted his head, smiling at the boy, but the kid looked away,

80

suddenly cold and distant as he tucked himself back into his pants.

Puzzled but unalarmed, Mike flicked the lights back on, started off again. "Take a left here," the kid told him, his voice unpleasant and harsh. Mike did so, uneasily aware of the change of mood.

"I oughta kick your ass for that," the kid snapped suddenly. Mike caught his breath. Nobody raped you, he wanted to say; you liked it as well as I did. But he caught himself. The kid was sore, looking for a scapegoat to justify what he had done so eagerly. Arguing would only make it worse.

"Pull over," the kid ordered. "I'd rather walk." Mike pulled obediently to the curb, hoping the kid would get out of the car before his anger erupted.

"You fucking queer," he suddenly snarled, his face vicious and ugly. He reached across the seat, grabbing Mike's jacket. The buttons tore lose in his grip; "Get out of this car and I'll break your rotten neck for you."

"Easy," Mike told him, trying to be calm. The kid was small but powerful looking, and angry enough to do just what he had threatened. "Look, I don't want any trouble, okay?"

The kid struck out and Mike ducked so that the blow barely grazed his chin. He tensed, raising his arm to ward off another blow and their eyes met for an instant. Disgust, hatred, violence—they were all there in the kid's eyes. He seemed about to strike again; then, with an oath, he opened the door and jumped from the car, slamming the door shut.

With a gasp of relief, Mike started off quickly, little caring whether the young man was free of the car or not. In the rear view mirror he saw the kid still standing there on the curb, cursing after him.

Morbidly silent, still shaken, Mike retraced his route, on his way once again to the *Why Not*. He could not stop thinking of the hot-blooded youth whose male beauty he had tasted in his mouth a very few minutes before. Mike had had many of them—the animal ones who agreed for the sake of sexual pleasure, too sure of their own manhood to fear contamination; the ones who regarded it as an honorable way of earning money; the innocents, virgins still, eager to explore the world of sexual experience beyond the door of masturbation.

But these, the ones like the kid who had just gotten out of the car, they were the dangerous ones, dangerous and strangely pathetic, already homosexual, fighting it with any weapon at their disposal. They came out, and hated themselves for it, and in time went on to murder, or suicide, always afraid to face the rotted truth within themselves: that they were, in the long run, the queers whom they professed to hate.

* * * * * * *

Les (it was really Sylvester, but no one called him that) Klein paused at the corner, in front of a darkened shop window, and pretended to examine the small display of merchandise beyond the glass. In reality, he was slowly, cautiously examining his own reflection, trying, without success, to see it as a stranger would see it.

THE *WHY NOT*, by Victor J. Banis

He started at the top, the hair a sandy brown, neither distinguished nor unpleasant. For a long time he had thought of dying his hair, maybe black. If it were black, he could dye the temples gray—at my age, they should be gray anyway, he told himself. That would give him a distinguished look. After all, when a man reaches forty, it isn't right for his hair to look so young. Maybe for some people, with those babyish, always young-looking faces; but his face wasn't babyish or young looking. It wasn't pretty enough for that.

"If I took off my glasses," he mused, but he quickly shook his head. He had tried that in the past, but he was almost literally blind without the thick, unattractive lenses in front of his eyes. He had tried contact lenses, but he had not been able to get used to them, and had given them up after a few weeks. Besides, he reminded himself, he had a face that went with glasses; everybody said so. The nose, definitely a Jewish nose, which he had been intending for a long time to have fixed; the full, too-fleshy mouth. No, the glasses added a needed touch of character.

He dropped his gaze, studying the shirt and trousers, the fourth outfit he had donned before coming out. They were, he concluded, the best choice after all. The dark shirt, the not-too-tight slacks, helped to minimize his plump and badly proportioned body. Definitely slimming, he thought, definitely flattering, just the right shade of brown to suit his coloring. He looked, he decided, unusually good. Tonight will be a good night, he promised himself, and moved away from the window, down the street.

THE *WHY NOT*, by Victor J. Banis

The sound of the music greeted him while he was still a distance from the door to the bar. He paused again, feeling the familiar discomfort, a fear that gripped him each time he came to one of these places. What if nothing happened? What if nobody, happened? Suppose someone laughed at him, or worse? Some of those queens were pretty bitchy. He had never been popular in gay circles. He did not have the necessary humor or wit, the hard to define charm, that x quality that bred success in these places.

I'll go home, he thought morosely, and turned to make his way back to his car. He reached the corner, changed his mind again, and hurried back to the open door with its billowing draperies and went in before he could change his mind again. Inside, he stood for a long moment, blinking his eyes to accustom them to the gloom. The place was packed, filled to overflowing with moving, wispy bodies.

I'll never get a drink, he thought desperately. He stood near the end of the bar, hoping somebody would leave and give access to the counter. No one did, and finally he leaned across the shoulders of two men, hoping they wouldn't say anything unpleasant to him. One of them half turned, giving him a surly glance, but he held his ground and ordered a beer from the bartender.

"Nice crowd," he commented as the bartender handed him his change, but the pretty blond had already directed his attention to another customer. Hurt by what he saw as a rebuff, Les shuffled away from the bar. He found a spot near a post where he could stand and watch the group at the pinball machine, trying to play their game despite the masses of bodies in their way. He studied one of the players, a beautiful young man in pale Levis and form-fitting tee shirt.

God, what I would give for something like that, he thought, just for one night; for one hour, even. He watched the curve of the delicately molded buttocks as the player bent over, admired the bulge of basket when a quick turn gave him a glimpse of it. He had never had anyone that beautiful in his life, except in his mind, phantoms that he conjured up as an incentive to his solitary pleasures.

He tore his eyes away, finally, determined not to torture himself with desire for anything so unattainable. Nearer to him a thin, nervous-acting queen was standing by himself, sipping a drink from the glass in his hand. No beauty, Les judged, examining the figure, but not so bad. Not so good either, of course. He was skinny, with a bad complexion, and sloppy in his appearance.

I'll bet he doesn't get too many offers, was the thought in Les' mind. But he looks intelligent. Intelligent people are always nervous. I'm always nervous. He tried to picture himself and the skinny queen together, talking earnestly and passionately about music, or art. I'm cultured, he reminded himself, and intelligent. He would probably like to know somebody like me.

The queen turned, caught Les staring at him. Les blushed, but forced himself to smile and not to look away. "You look lonely," he said aloud, although in little more than a whisper. The queen stared back, moved a step closer. He likes me, Les thought with delight, his smile growing larger.

"I couldn't hear you," the young queen said, his expression blank and unpromising.

"I said," Les stammered, embarrassed by his own obvious interest. "I said you look lonely." The queen looked him up and down.

"Not really," he said in a dry tone.

Maybe he's being coy, Les thought without much hope. "Can I buy you a drink?"

"No, thanks." The queen turned away, turned his back on him, and moved off, blending into the crowd. Les felt his face burning scarlet, stinging as though he had been slapped. He moved away himself, wondering if anybody nearby had heard the exchange. He kept moving, circling the bar, sipping his beer and watching the faces as he passed. Some of them looked back, searching his for an instant.

Yes, yes, I'll care, he wanted to scream. I will trade with you, caring for caring, affection for affection. Your search, my search, they are over now. But he did not scream or speak, nor did the passing faces. He set his bottle, empty now, on the bar and shuffled to the rear, to the restroom. A flighty-looking faggot came in while he was standing at the urinal and Les caught the faggot's eyes on him. I am hung, he told himself proudly. If nothing else, I'm big, and isn't that what they all like in the long run? He lifted his eyes to the faggot's, and smiled into the mirror. The faggot looked blankly back, without smiling, and left the restroom.

Again Les looked at himself, this time in the mirror over the washbasin. "I'm ugly," he said aloud, and knew that it was the truth. He looked not unlike a giant frog, a fat, ugly queen, growing less attractive as he grew older.

86

THE *WHY NOT*, by Victor J. Banis

He forgot to wash his hands. He did not stop for another beer, but made his way as quickly as the crowds allowed to the front door and left. Don't think, he told himself as he climbed into his car and began the drive home. It doesn't matter. Ugly people find lovers, too. I'll find someone eventually. I'll find an ugly lover. Don't think.

Once home, he stripped, tossing his clothes carelessly about the bedroom of his large and elegant apartment. Still trying to keep his mind a blank, he threw himself numbly down upon the sheets of the bed, flicking the light out.

In the dark, he thought again of the boy in the pale Levis. He closed his eyes, trying to remember every detail of the lithe, graceful body, the innocent, radiant face. His hands went instinctively to his crotch. In his imagination he felt the soft, warm body of his dream next to his own, curving buttocks pressed against his thighs. His hand had begun to move, faster and faster, just as in his vision their bodies, made one now, moved faster and faster, building to a climax of sensation.

The sheet will be wet, he thought angrily. He hated the sheet wet.

10:02 PM
Saturday Night

◄Chapter Three►

Clara frowned as the insistent, blaring sound of a rock and roll record spewed from the radio behind her. She was sorry that she had come—such crude people, not at all her sort.

Of course it was Agatha's doing. She was always taking up with the strangest ones—and she did owe Agatha a favor, something to make up for not inviting her to the party. How in the hell had she found out about it, anyway? Jackie, probably—that girl couldn't keep anything secret. It was most unlikely that Agatha really believed she had been invited, despite Clara's insistence. No, she knew very well that she had not been, and no doubt she would find some opportunity to gain her vengeance.

In the meantime, Clara thought dismally, here I am in this awful house, with just the sort of people I cannot bear, and Agatha certainly is not going to want to leave, not for hours yet.

Agatha indeed was at that moment pouring herself another drink from the bottles scattered on the makeshift bar. She stirred the drink with her finger and glided across the room to where Clara sat on the sofa in the corner.

"What the hell are you doing in this dark corner alone, girl?" Agatha demanded. "Or do you have somebody hidden under the cushions?"

THE *WHY NOT*, by Victor J. Banis

"Oh, I'm having a breather," Clara apologized, making room for her sister on the seat beside her. "I'm getting to be an old woman, pet. I can't carry on the way you do."

"Carry on!" Agatha shrieked with delight, clearly pleased to think that she could out-go her companion. "Well, what do you think God made queens for, pray tell me? Did you get a load of the piece of chicken Larry brought around? Do you think it's his trick, or just an ornament he carried over for all to see?"

"If it is his trick, somebody will get an evil throat cut before the night is over," Clara said. "Or haven't you noticed? Miss sweet young thing is doing everything but sixty-nine with that other one, the German."

Agatha followed the meaningful glance and giggled happily. "Mercy, what a pair! Wouldn't you just love to be in the middle? Madge, I would be out of my mind."

"You are out of your fruit mind, love, you and your group therapy. Besides, they don't look like they need you."

Agatha frowned at that, and took another swallow of her drink. "It could be arranged, never you worry about that. I'll bet it wouldn't take much to get a daisy chain going." She smacked her lips, smiling again. "As a matter of fact, that's not a bad idea. You know how Kurt loves his dirty pictures."

"For crap's sake, you wouldn't let him take pictures of you? He'll have them tacked up in every tearoom in town."

THE *WHY NOT,* by Victor J. Banis

Agatha's expression left little doubt that she would most certainly allow her picture to be taken. "Well, count me out," Clara concluded lamely.

"Oh, woman, I'll bet you douche with vinegar, sour as you are," Agatha stormed, jumping up from the sofa to march off across the room. She went, Clara observed, directly to Kurt. The evening, from Clara's point of view, was certainly becoming a dismal thing.

"Hi," someone said over her.

She looked up to find one of her hosts—what were their names?—smiling down at her. Not a bad-looking number, for that rather vulgar type. She smiled back, wondering if she should invite him to sit down. She didn't stand a chance with him, she was sure of that. He was the playboy type, could have anything he wanted, and probably cold as an iceberg to boot. That type usually was.

"You look lonely," he decided, giving her a mock frown. "How about a dance?"

The music from the radio had become a slow, heady number, loud and insistent but with a more sultry mood than the boisterous racket of a moment ago. Smiling demurely, Clara stood, melting into his arms. He is strong, she thought appreciatively, leaning daintily against him. You would never know if he was gay, meeting him on the street. Maybe he's not, she added with some concern. These people were just the sort to be inviting rough trade in. But of course, that was silly. Rough trade wouldn't be dancing with her, holding her close the way he was.

The music ended. For a second they remained together; then, slowly, they separated. His eyes were twinkling as he pulled her back to him, kissed her hotly on the mouth.

He likes me, she thought with a sudden hysterical happiness. My God, this doll likes me.

Whatever he might have said when they separated was lost in the scream from the adjoining room. "Come, come," somebody was shouting. "They're having a daisy chain and Kurt's taking pictures."

Her young man moved at once toward the laughter and merriment. Still clinging to him, Clara held back. "Must we?" she asked, wanting to stay here with him, wanting him to kiss her again.

"Come on," he insisted, pulling his hand free from hers. "This should be fun."

Without waiting for her, he left, disappearing into the group standing at the doorway. Angry and hurt, Clara considered returning to her sofa but her mood of solitude was broken now and she drifted idly in the direction of the reported daisy chain.

Just as she had expected, Agatha was in the middle of everything. The damn dirt bag had managed to get in between the cute young couple after all, and there they were, the three of them, stark naked on the floor, their bodies forming an unbroken circle. On a nearby ladder, Kurt was busy taking flash pictures from above.

Disgusting, Clara decided, although she made no attempt to leave the scene. She had to admit that the young one was beautiful. And, she decided, he sure as hell was no virgin.

While they watched, the German's head bobbed up. "Got enough pictures?" he yelled up to Kurt.

THE *WHY NOT*, by Victor J. Banis

"Don't stop now," Kurt insisted, fitting another flashbulb into the camera. "I've got half a dozen to go yet."

"Well, you better take them fast," the German suggested. That produced a fresh wave of laughter and some choice comments from the onlookers.

Clara was aware of some activity behind her and turned to see her dancing partner and two others busily gathering up the clothes that the three on the floor had removed. He held up a finger to his lips and winked at Clara as the three of them hid the clothes carefully behind a chair. On his way past Clara, he stopped and whispered, "We're going to give them a scare. Charlie is going to come around the outside of the house and bang on the door."

Despite herself, Clara could barely suppress a laugh of delight as she waited for the fun to begin. It would give that old trollop, Agatha, a well-deserved lesson.

The banging on the front door was loud enough to bring all the noise in the room to a halt. The three on the floor jumped up in alarm as Clara's young man, looking genuinely startled, hurried to a window at the front of the house and pulled a drape aside. "It's the Law," he hissed, his eyes wide. "Clean it up."

The scramble that followed was almost more than the conspirators could bear. Clara laughed harder than anyone as she watched the three nudes dashing about the room looking for their clothes. The youngest flew up the stairs to seek a hiding place there, while the German made a rather futile attempt at hiding himself behind a drapery that stuck stubbornly out in front of him.

By this time the others present had tumbled to the gag, and the laughter brought the German sheepishly from behind the drape. Someone went for the young boy and he pranced back down the stairs, sharing in the general mirth and posing to show off his nudity.

"Where's Agatha?" someone wanted to know. Clara remembered seeing her scrambling about the room looking for her lost clothes, but then she had become interested in the plight of the German and had lost track of her sister.

"My God, she may have killed herself," someone suggested.

"Not her," Clara assured them, and they began to look about in the various rooms for the missing queen. Someone noticed finally that the bathroom door was closed and pushed it boldly open to reveal Agatha herself, still naked, standing before the mirror and busily repairing her eye make-up.

"She's making herself pretty for the paddy-wagon!" someone shrieked, and this caused more laughter.

"You dizzy cow!" Clara snorted, glowering at her friend. "There ain't any police here. Come out of that john and get your clothes on before you catch cold."

"Balls," Agatha snapped, emerging from the bathroom. "And I thought we were in for some real excitement."

* * * * * * *

The ringing of the phone brought Sandy out of his bed in one quick movement, wishing as he hurried into the living room that he had gotten an extension. He banged his leg against the corner of the desk in the dark, but managed to pick up the receiver before the third ring.

"Sandy?" The voice at the other end of the line was male, deep and husky, and not familiar.

"Yes?" Sandy shook his head, trying to wake himself up from the deep sleep in which he had been. "Who is this?" My God, it was eleven o'clock at night. Who would be calling at this hour?

"You don't know me," the voice explained rapidly—a nice voice, pleasantly masculine, comfortable. "A friend gave me your number, he said you and I should get together sometime."

A friend—odd, Sandy couldn't imagine who would be giving out his phone number that way. In the distance, faintly, he could hear the sound of music, and an occasional voice. A party, he thought; somebody was at a party, and this was just a gag. "Where are you?" he asked, hoping maybe to recognize the voice after all.

"I'm at the Why Not. You've been here before, haven't you?"

Sandy hesitated. He had been there, all right. Who hadn't? But this might be a trick—the police, maybe, trying to trick him into admitting something. He had heard they did that, got phone numbers, called people, set up meetings, which turned into arrests.

"Maybe," he hedged, growing nervous. "Who gave you the number?"

"Just a friend," the voice said. "He told me you liked big men, if you know what I mean."

THE *WHY NOT*, by Victor J. Banis

Sandy gasped, startled by the bluntness of the insinuation. Who the hell would say that kind of thing on the telephone, to a stranger? It must be the police, or else it was some kind of nut. Maybe even an out-and-out lunatic. "There must be some mistake...." he said. His throat went dry.

The voice on the other end chuckled, a low, throaty sound. "I'll bet you would like what I have got in my hand right now," he said. "Man, am I hot. You really ought to see me. I am as hard as a rock. Doesn't it make you hot, just thinking about it?"

Yes, oddly enough, it was making him hot, the description that was continuing, becoming increasingly graphic. This is crazy, Sandy told himself, his hands shaking. It's just some nut, talking dirty on the telephone. Sane people don't do this sort of thing. The man couldn't be sane.

"Baby, I hear you are sweeter than heaven," an insinuating whisper. "I would love to see you. Wouldn't you like that too? Wouldn't you like to spend the night with me beside you?"

"No," Sandy whispered hoarsely, squirming uncomfortably in his chair. He was getting aroused from all this. How long had it been for him, months now? He wanted someone so desperately, but not like this, not something so dangerous. This man was crazy. He might do anything. He fought himself weakly, wanting to hang up, bring this conversation to an end; but he was mesmerized by the low, exciting voice that droned on, calling to mind scenes of sexual abandon.

The voice chuckled again. "Don't kid me, baby, you'd give your right arm for me right now, wouldn't you? Come on, tell me the truth. I'll bet you are all excited just thinking about it. I'll bet you are hard too, aren't you?"

"Yes," Sandy whispered hoarsely. I shouldn't admit that, he told himself, his temples throbbing. It will only encourage him. I should hang up right now—but he'll only call back, won't he? Oh, God, what do people do about these things?

"Your buddy says you really like it. He says you have got a hot little backside. I would love to find out for myself. I'd love to get to know you, you know that? You would never forget it, I promise you. Look, are you home alone?"

Sandy groaned, his mind whirling madly about inside his head. "Yes," he gasped into the receiver. "But I won't...."

"Your buddy gave me the address. He said you'd be home alone tonight, just dreaming of someone like me. Ten minutes, okay? I can be there in ten minutes."

Sandy tried to say something, anything, but the words wouldn't come, and a moment later the connection was broken, the phone humming ominously in his ear.

"He won't really come," he told himself, hanging up the receiver. "It's just a gag, somebody at a party trying to upset me." He thought of something else: the Why Not was far more than ten minutes away. That had been a lie.

He hurried back to the bedroom, turning on the light, and dashed wildly about, suddenly determined to dress and go out before the caller got here—if he even really was on his way. His socks, he discovered as he tied his shoelaces, didn't match.

THE *WHY NOT*, by Victor J. Banis

"Oh, hell," he muttered, leaving them as they were. He was pulling a sweater over his head when the doorbell rang. It hadn't been ten minutes, surely, more like five. He thought of the pay phone down the street, a block and a half away. He must have been there, that must have been where he was calling from. But why had he lied about it?

He groaned aloud, genuinely frightened now, and crouched against the wall as though he might be seen through the doors and walls between them. The bell rang persistently, loudly.

Finally, there was a silence. Sandy flicked off the light, found himself a cigarette and lit it, trying to calm his shaking hands. A minute later the doorbell started again. Feverishly he stubbed out the cigarette in the ashtray by the bed. His hand went instinctively to his sex, as though to protect or comfort it.

The doorbell continued to ring for a long time.

* * * * * * *

Midnight—by now they are all here, their voices pitched higher than ever in a vain attempt to carry over the roar of the crowd, their movements, far from subdued by the confining crush of bodies, grown all the more frantic and uninhibited.

Nicky is holding forth on a stool at the bar, to the obvious displeasure of Jackie, and drunkenly buying drinks for the house, seeking to achieve in his burst of munificence some bit of flair, succeeding only in being loud and foolish. I decline the drink he offers me and he turns his back on me, attempting to be, in his sarcasm, cutting; to repay my disdain with humiliation. But I laugh at him and move away, bored by his futile wit.

Lady Agatha and Clara have descended, swept into this chamber of sorrow with loud laughter and delightfully degenerate accounts of their evening: orgies with naked bodies sprawled about the floors, countless men falling at their painted feet. Agatha's eyes search the bar all the while she talks, watching carefully for a response to her probing gaze.

Ralph and Joe sit at a table, uncomfortably separating themselves from the spirit of the night and the place—Joe gazing with frustrated longing at a little blond near the bar, Ralph trying to conceal his own interest in a basket dangerously close to his face, the two of them smiling frequently at one another. They should go home, I think. I start toward them, wanting to tell them to leave, but I check myself. They will leave soon enough, perhaps made stronger by this interval of weakness. They will no longer need to wonder what they are missing and can be grateful for what they have, this night no more than a fleeting interlude in the riptide of their lives, a moment of calm in an eternity of turmoil. Soon, too soon, it will be ended, something on which to look back sadly, these times together to be remembered as they stand alone on some future night and wonder what went wrong. Let them drink, I tell myself, drink and cruise and hurry home to their shared bed, to find in one another the answer to their misery. A brief answer? Then, at least, let it be a sweet one.

THE *WHY NOT*, by Victor J. Banis

The hustler—he is a hustler, I know for certain—speaking in all too warm and pleasant tones to Rich. I might warn Rich, tell him that others have explored that route before him, only to find ugliness and filth for the promised splendor. But no, he would not believe that this charming and gracious creature before him, so polite, so thoughtful—lighting a cigarette for him, a real gentleman—will turn soon enough into a monster. He would argue that I want it for myself, and perhaps I do. Danger or no danger, or perhaps because of the danger, there is attraction there, an animal appeal, and perhaps I would do as Rich will do, leave with him, take him home, hope that the act is not an act at all.

Mark, collegiate, handsome, fragile but not effeminate, has already been selected, and selected a companion, someone who will leave with him soon, hurry away to that darkened house, lie with him in the night and try to be careful, quiet so that Mother will not hear, although Mother has already heard it before, has too often turned her face to her bedroom wall in a stubborn attempt to blot out the sounds from her son's bedroom.

Les is here now, wandering timidly about, seeking a kind face and finding no one. I promise myself to speak to him, offer him a drink but he is across the room, too far for me to walk just now, for I have seen a smile, a pair of eyes meeting mine, asking an eternal question—a pretty face, smiling hopefully, a face, perhaps, to find on my pillow in the morning.

But it is early yet. The excitement, the frivolity of the night is at its peak. This is the hour for fun and laughter and loud conversation. As the hour passes and the night draws to its end, there will be time for meeting, for selecting. But for now the show goes on. It is better for the moment to watch, to see the drama unfold.

Dennis, quiet, not so much lonely as alone, preparing to leave by himself, ignoring the man at the bar—vice, I am sure of it—who has been cruising him, who follows him out into the street.

Lynn—new still, and by rights entitled to a certain attention—but too alone, too determinedly seated at his table, watching the door, waiting for someone to enter—a friend perhaps, or maybe it is his destiny he awaits.

A hand in passing gropes me, squeezing my crotch furtively and a pair of eyes meet mine in the mirror, but mine remain guarded, not encouraging, and they go on to be replaced by a hundred others.

* * * * * * *

Rich found his hand trembling slightly as he leaned toward the match, inhaled deeply, and smiled at the roughly good-looking man in front of him.

"Whew, this place is getting jammed," he commented, hopeful that the hint would be taken, followed up. He wanted desperately to leave with this exciting stranger, go on together to a more intimate situation. But his natural timidity held him back from asking directly, his timidity and his acquired reserve. This was, after all, a stranger, terribly masculine acting, although unquestionably friendly. Better to let him make the first move, better that he should affirm that he was genuinely interested. It was safer that way, fascinating blue eyes or no fascinating blue eyes.

"Yeah, it is," the blond stranger agreed, glancing briefly about the bar. "I am never comfortable around crowds."

Was that a hint, or not? It could be an invitation, or again maybe just an idle comment. He had a pretty smile, thin lips, German descent most likely. "I usually enjoy drinking at home," Rich said. "I prefer that. At least, when there is someone with me." There, he couldn't mistake that. If he's interested....

"Got anything there to drink?"

He was interested. Rich smiled warmly, too excited to pretend otherwise. "Sure. Want to come by for a while?"

And it was settled. A torturously long period while they finished their drinks. Rich afraid every moment that someone else might catch his eye or interfere, someone more attractive. Maybe he is only being polite, he thought, trying frantically to follow the blond's gaze about the room. He may not want anything more than that drink. Maybe he is not even gay. He was unquestionably masculine. But he's been so friendly. Was he staring at Jackie? Oh, God, what if he likes Jackie better?

Finally the drinks were finished. They started out, Rich smugly proud to be seen leaving with such a beauty, confident that others were watching him enviously. Outside, he wished the queens in the bar could see him getting into the stranger's car. It was a new Thunderbird! Real class.

Leaning back in the seat, Rich allowed himself to drift lightly off into a series of dreams,

THE *WHY NOT*, by Victor J. Banis

dreams in which the rugged blond beside him declared his undying love, dreams in which they came home from their respective jobs in an evening to embrace one another, long lovely nights together. Could this be the one, the one he had been searching for, the one for a lifetime? So many tries, so many failures. But maybe this time....

He sat upright in his seat, thrusting the dreams brutally aside. This one might not be the marrying kind. He might have a lover already and this could be just a fleeting diversion. Better make the most of the moment, of the night, and see what happens.

"This is it," he said aloud, pointing to a large apartment house ahead. "Better park in front."

He wondered as they parked and entered the building, climbing the stairs to his apartment, if the stranger was impressed. It was a nice building— garish, too Hollywood, but nice. More expensive, really than he could afford, but impressive for tricks, with its pool, the Birds-of-Paradise in their planters, the palm leaves waving lazily at them. It was impossible, though, to tell if the stranger was impressed, his expression was impassive.

Once inside his apartment he found himself uncomfortably ill at ease. What to do now? He had never been good at these things. He could never bring himself to be blunt enough for the occasion. What would this one prefer, the direct approach— would you like to go to bed? He couldn't imagine himself saying anything that direct.

"How about some coffee?" he asked instead, hoping that perhaps his companion might break the ice for them.

"Sure," the blond answered, seating himself stiffly on one end of the sofa. He's cooler, more distant, Rich fretted as he put on the water for the coffee. He's nervous too, and not nearly so friendly as he was at the bar.

He continued to worry as he made two cups of coffee—instant, it was all he had—and carried them into the living room. The stranger was still in the same spot on the sofa, saying nothing. He's lost interest, Rich told himself dismally, setting one cup on the small table—a Goodwill purchase, but still in nice condition. He carried his own cup to the other end, wanting to sit close but afraid of being pushy. He sipped the coffee, nervously fingering a thread hanging loose from the sofa. "This poor old sofa," he commented, indicating the loose thread. "It has seen better days."

"Yeah," the stranger said without even looking. He was, Rich thought, downright sullen now. He tried vainly to think of anything he might have said or done to irritate his guest. "I bought it second hand, three years ago, so I guess I can't complain.

Still no comment. He hadn't even touched the coffee. "Would you like to stay the night?" Maybe he was the impatient kind; maybe the direct approach would have been better.

"Why not?" the stranger responded, still seemingly quite uninterested. He was lost, to all appearances, in some other world of his own, scarcely aware of Rick's presence or comments.

"You could sleep in my room," Rich offered hopefully "Or I can bring some blankets out and you could sleep here on the couch. It's not very comfortable...."

THE *WHY NOT*, by Victor J. Banis

"This will be fine," the blond told him, a note of finality in his voice. "I won't need any blankets."

He was looking at Rich now and Rich was painfully aware that something was expected of him, but not at all sure just what. Did the man want him to sleep out here too, or did he want to be alone? So strange, so different from the way he had been in the bar.

"Well, I'll let you get to sleep," he said unhappily. He half stood, switched off the light by the couch. Then, bolder in the darkness, he stretched out one hand, allowed it to rest lightly on the stranger's knees. "Do you want anything before I go to bed?"

There was a silence, a long silence before the stranger said, "Turn the light back on."

Obediently, miserably unhappy, Rich reached for the light and turned it on again He turned back to the stranger and his eyes opened wide in alarm. He was looking into the barrel of a gun, a revolver of some sort.

The blond stood quickly, menacing him with the gun. "Okay, let's have it—your billfold." He held out his hand, closing and opening his fingers.

This can't be happening, Rich told himself, reaching at once for his billfold. He was so nice at the bar, so charming. It must be a joke. He tried to smile but the situation wasn't at all funny. "There isn't much left," he said hoarsely, handing the billfold over.

"Seven lousy bucks," the blond snarled, flinging the billfold to the floor. "Don't fuck around with me. Where's the rest of it?"

"That's all there is," Rich whined, still sitting tensely on the end of the sofa. He's going to kill me,

105

he thought frantically. I'm going to die. And he was so nice at the bar.

"Come here." Obediently, Rich stood, walked on unsteady legs toward him. A hand shot out, striking him across the cheek, and he reeled backward, almost fell.

"There isn't any more," he sobbed. He closed his eyes, waiting for another blow, or a shot.

The blond was quiet for a moment, so that Rich reopened his eyes. "What else you got around here?"

"There—there isn't much," Rich stammered, barely able to speak. "You're welcome to whatever you want. I have some jewelry, cheap stuff mostly, but you can have it. And my watch—here, take my watch."

He pulled the watch roughly off his wrist, dropped it on the sofa. The blond picked it up, examined it, and sneered as he threw it back on the sofa. "Let's see the rest of it."

Rich led the way into the bedroom, conscious every second of the gun following him. There was nothing there of any value. At the blond's instructions he emptied the drawers of his dresser on the floor, wondering if the neighbors would hear the noise, and come to investigate.

The blond was growing angrier, plainly disappointed in his profits. He stood frozen, the gun still pointed at Rich.

"My checkbook," Rich said suddenly, seeing it on the floor at his feet and seizing upon the thought. "I could write you a check."

"Fat chance I'd have of cashing it," the blond answered with another sneer, fingering the gun impatiently.

"We could cash it tonight," Rich hurried on, clinging tenaciously to this one hope. "There's an all-night market near here. I shop there a lot. They may cash it for me."

The blond was interested, giving the possibility some consideration. "Where's the checkbook? Make it for a hundred," he instructed when Rich had retrieved the checkbook from the debris on the floor.

It was more than Rich had in the bank, twice as much, but that did not matter now. He could borrow the rest to cover the check in the morning—if he lived that long. If he didn't, it really wouldn't matter, would it? But for the present the blond was calmer, less vicious acting.

"Remember," the blond told him as they started from the apartment. "I have the gun under my shirt. Any funny business and I can let you have it before they could stop me, okay?"

Rich nodded, all too aware of the truth of the statement. Fat lot of good it would do him if they caught this one after he was dead. Heroics were out, that was for certain.

* * * * * * *

The night manager, it seemed, was off. "Isn't there anyone else who can cash this for me," Rich argued, frightened anew by the unexpected complication. "Didn't he leave anyone in charge?"

"Sure, but I can't cash a check that big. I'm not even saying he will, but I can't. He will be back in an hour, if you want to try then."

The blond however seemed to take the delay calmly. "Let's find someplace and have some coffee," he suggested when they back in the car. Rich thought of the coffee at his apartment, but he felt somehow safer out in public, not so trapped despite the gun still under the blond's shirt.

They found an all night coffee shop nearby. There was no reminder, this time, of the gun. They entered the shop together, took seats at the counter. Rich glanced into the mirror behind the counter, almost amused by their reflections. They looked so ordinary; two friends stopping on their way home for a final cup of coffee.

"I don't have any money," he said suddenly, the irony of the fact even more amusing. Even the blond grinned, a pleasant grin. "I'll treat," he said.

The waitress came, brought them coffee, and left. Rich's head had begun to throb painfully and his shoulder ached. But he was still alive, and the blond beside him was offering him a cigarette in an astonishingly friendly gesture.

"You know, you've been pretty nice about all this," he said, lighting Rich's cigarette for him.

"I don't want to give you any trouble," Rich answered, hoping it was the right thing to say. So strange, the blond was almost as he had been in the bar earlier: pleasant, charming, harmless-looking.

"Look...." The blond dropped his eyes to his coffee, steaming in its cup. "I'm sorry I slugged you. I was sore. No hard feelings, okay?"

THE *WHY NOT*, by Victor J. Banis

No hard feelings? Rich suppressed a desire to laugh. He had been struck, was being robbed, frightened out of his wits, might still be killed before this was over—no hard feelings?

"It's all right," he said aloud, afraid to risk any further anger. Then, impulsively, he asked, "Do you do this often?"

"No." He seemed unperturbed by the question. "I needed some money bad." He paused. "This ever happen to you before?"

"No." Rich shook his head. "Never."

"Look, you ought to know how to take care of yourself. Ever do any fighting?"

Rich's eyes widened and he half thought it was meant as a joke, but his companion appeared serious. "No," he answered, remaining serious himself. "I don't know how. I'm too thin...."

"Ah, three, four weeks, we could put some meat on your bones. I could have you in real shape in a couple of months, teach you how to use your fists."

Rich was too astonished to make a reply. That beats everything, he told himself, staring into the blond's eyes. And he is serious. He is trying to be nice, really trying.

"What you need is someone to look after you, teach you to be a man."

"Yes, I suppose so." What the hell could one say in such a situation? "I've never had anyone...."

"Well, I'll tell you what. When this is all over, maybe the two of us can get together. You're okay. Honest, I mean it. If you really want some help, I'll work with you. But I am warning you, I

will make you work. You'll have to cut down on
those cigarettes, too, for starters."

Rich nodded his head slowly, self-
consciously putting his cigarette out. He felt somehow moved by the offer—such a strange situation,
and yet, he would like someone to…. "I'd like that,"
he said softly.

They finished their coffee and drove back to
the store. It took some time for Rich to convince the
night manager to cash the check—family emer-
gency, he explained; he wanted to leave right away.
Finally to his relief the manager relented, gave him
the cash. Weak from the tension, Rich led the way
from the store, wanting to run, as though in some
mysterious way the manager might discover that the
check was no good.

Outside he handed the money to his companion, aware that it was a crucial moment. Would the
guy decide after all to kill him? Or would he pursue
his plans to make a "man" of Rich? "Don't worry
about the police," Rich said quickly. "I won't report
this. You don't have to worry about any trouble."

"Come on," the blond told him, indicating the
car. They started off again, driving back in the direction of Rich's apartment. On his side of the seat
Rich held his breath, expecting at every corner that
they would turn into one of the darker and less trav-
eled side streets. But they drove straight back, all
the way to the apartment, and parked in the same
spot as before.

"How about that coffee now?" his companion
suggested, sliding out of the car on the driver's side.
Puzzled, and frightened anew, Rich got out his own
side, led the way once again up the stairs to the

110

apartment, so different from the time before. Had he been brought home only to be killed here? That was silly, surely. There were much safer places for that. Here the neighbors might hear. Still….

He put the water on again for coffee, came back to the living room, where the blond was sitting as before on the sofa, as if they were replaying the earlier scene. As least the gun was not on display. Rich seated himself stiffly in the chair across the room; very tired now and wishing he could go to sleep.

"I feel like a heel," the blond said, breaking the silence between them. Rich wanted to laugh, but his fear checked him. He felt like a heel? It was really quite silly, the whole business. "It's all right," he said aloud. "Don't worry about it."

"No, I mean you brought me up here expecting something. You wanted sex, didn't you?"

Rich started, surprised by the question. It was the last thing he had expected to hear at this point in the evening. Surely he could not want…I couldn't, he told himself, not after….

"No, that's all right," he insisted, shaking his head. "It's no fun when—when the other person doesn't want it. I don't like it when—unless I know it's being enjoyed." He stopped, staring as the blond rubbed himself meaningfully.

"Come here," he said, his voice low and husky.

"It's all right, really," Rich argued. The thought of sex, after the nightmare he had been through, was appalling.

"I'll like it," the blond assured him. "Come on, come here."

111

THE *WHY NOT*, by Victor J. Banis

There was nothing for Rich to do but stand and cross the room. Kneeling nervously on the floor. He thought of the gun, still tucked in the belt beneath the shirt so far as he knew. From the kitchen he could hear the water whistling in the kettle.

It's dirty, he thought with a shudder as he tugged it out of the trousers. His head moved, his eyes closed, waiting tensely for the telltale symptoms: a stiffening of the legs, an upward thrust of the hips.

He breathed deeply, glad when it was over, remaining on his knees for a moment before rising. The blond was already zipping his trousers. "Thanks," he said simply.

"The water's hot," Rich said, wanting to vomit and afraid that he would be sick any minute.

"Forget it," the blond said, standing. He gave his crotch a final, paternal pat. "Get some sleep."

Rich watched anxiously as he crossed the room to the door, turned the knob. It was over. He was leaving, and Rich was still alive.

"I'll stop by tonight," the blond said, his tone one that allowed for no objection. "About seven or so. Maybe we can go to a movie, okay?"

Rich nodded, afraid to disagree. The door opened, permitting entrance to a welcome burst of cool night air, and he was gone.

* * * * * * *

Ken Grabman, busy at the fine art of petting, listened with one corner of his attention to the sounds from the front seat of the car. He was, in fact, rather bored with the girl in his arms and the evening in general, but at the same time determined not to be a square. If Jess and Marta, locked together in the front seat, went all the way, Ken was prepared to do the same with Carol. On the other hand, he would as soon say good night to the girls, drop them off, and call it a night.

He smothered a sigh of relief as he saw Marta's head straighten and loom before them. Their necking session was over for the evening and he and Carol would be expected to take their cue.

His final kiss was a torrid one; no sense in disappointing Carol. Next time he might be more in the mood, and he preferred that she think he was mad with longing for her.

A few more brief exchanges, a lingering clasp of hands, and the girls were out of the car, going up the walk to the porch of Marta's house. The front door opened and closed, and the porch light went out. Ken slipped from the back seat of the car to take his place beside Jess in front and they drove away.

"I thought I had it made that time," Jess commented, wiping his hand across his mouth to rub away the traces of lipstick. "You never know with her whether she's going to put out or not."

"It's easier with Carol," Ken informed him, smiling what he hoped was a rueful smile. "She's not. At least not so far."

"Hell, why bother? You can get better than that. Why don't I fix you up with Sue's kid sister next week? She's a real hot number."

THE *WHY NOT*, by Victor J. Banis

"Great," Ken agreed, without any real enthusiasm. Why am I so bored with it all, he wondered to himself? He had no real interest in it any more.

"You feeling okay?" Jess took advantage of a stop sign to turn in Ken's direction. "You've been pretty quiet the whole evening."

Ken smiled, genuinely pleased with the concern in his buddy's voice. It was great, having a friend like Jess, someone who worried about you and looked out for you.

"Ah, I'm just in some kind of mood," he apologized. "I don't know what it is." He leaned across the seat and patted Jess' long, muscular leg to emphasize his remark. His hand lingered for a fraction of a second, sensing the current of strength in the limb beneath his hand. What a build, he thought enviously. He pulled his hand quickly but regretfully away.

Two figures appeared at the curb ahead, their arms extended into the street, thumbs raised. Jess shot a questioning glance at Ken and when he nodded, slowed the car for the two hitchhikers. Ken held the seat forward and the two clambered into the back seat.

"Going far?" one of them asked. The voice was nasal and grating, annoying to Ken in some way he did not quite understand.

"All the way to Santa Monica," Jess answered, starting up again.

They rode for a few blocks in silence, Ken lost in his own thoughts, idle thoughts of himself and Jess and the good times they had had together.

"You two out on the town?" one of the pair in the back seat asked.

114

THE *WHY NOT*, by Victor J. Banis

"Sort of," Jess answered. "We were, anyway. We just dropped our dates off."

"Did you make out?" the nasal voice asked. Ken jumped, startled by the bluntness of the question.

None of your fucking business, he almost said, but Jess had already laughed, that soft caressing laugh of his, and answered, "No. No luck tonight."

"That's a pity, a couple of good-looking things like you, getting all worked up for nothing. I'll bet you are all hot and bothered now, aren't you?"

"Not really," Ken answered coldly, speaking before Jess had a chance to answer. He was already aware of what they were leading up to and had determined not to encourage them. Jess had said nothing but he was smiling, amused by the situation—or by Ken's discomfort, it was hard to say which.

"This is the place," the nasal voice said, pointing ahead. "Ever been here?"

Ken instinctively leaned toward the window, took in the faded red front and half lighted neon that said *The Why Not*. "I don't think so," Jess was saying.

"Maybe we could buy you a drink?" one of them asked as they got out of the car. "You might enjoy yourselves."

"Thanks, but we're too young to be served in bars," Ken informed them quickly, again not giving Jess a chance to answer. He knew as well as Jess that the false identification they carried would get them served, the way it always had. He knew too that Jess was game enough to accept the invitation, just for laughs.

"Well, ta ta, and thanks for the lift, sweets." With sly giggles, the two swished off down the street. Ken looked back as the car pulled away, saw them enter the bar with a final wave.

"Hey, you are in a mood, aren't you," Jess said with another chuckle. His hand came over, squeezing Ken's shoulder playfully.

"I just don't like fairies," Ken answered, regretting immediately the sharpness of his tone. "I'm sorry," he apologized quickly.

"It's okay. I was just having some fun. Are you staying over at my place?"

"Yeah, I told the folks I'd be at your house tonight." It was a custom that they spent the night together after their dates—usually at Jess', less frequently at Ken's, where they had to share one large bedroom with Ken's little brother.

Jess' parents were already in bed when they arrived at his house. The two moved about the house quietly and respectfully, helping themselves to milk and cookies in the kitchen before turning out the lights and making their way to the stairs.

"My grandparents are visiting," Jess whispered as they went up the stairs, careful to make as little noise as possible. "They're sleeping in my room. We'll have to use Laura's room."

Ken started, grateful for the darkness that concealed his surprise. Laura's room was smaller than Jess', dominated by one double bed. He wasn't used to sleeping in the same bed with anyone. Jess' room had twin beds. So did his own room at home, with a cot for those occasions when Jess stayed

116

over. But one double bed, another body in the same bed with him? He knew he would not sleep well at all. If only Jess had mentioned this sooner.

"We could go over to my house," he offered lamely as Jess led the way into his sister's room, vacant while Laura was away at college. "I've got the cot, you know. We wouldn't have to crowd up."

"Ah, this will be fine," Jess assured him, closing the door behind him as he switched on the light. The bed seemed to Ken an overpowering presence, filling the space before them. Uncomfortable at the sight of it, Ken seated himself for a moment at the chair by the desk, delaying the necessity of crawling beneath the clean, neat sheets.

"Need the bathroom?" Jess asked, seemingly unaware of his friend's discomfort. When Ken shook his head, Jess slipped out with a whispered, "Be back in a minute."

Ken stood as the door closed and undressed hurriedly, borrowing hangers from the closet for his clothes. Despite his nervousness, he took time to hang everything neatly. He was in bed by the time Jess returned, the sheet pulled modestly up about his neck.

"Hey, you must be beat," Jess commented, standing at the foot of the bed to smile down at his friend.

Ken faked a yawn. "Yeah, I guess so."

"Well, now that you mention it, I'm ready for some sleep myself," Jess decided. He lifted his arms over his head, stretching lazily. Ken watched the T-shirt lift upward with the gesture, revealing a narrow strip of bare stomach and the hollow of a navel.

THE *WHY NOT*, by Victor J. Banis

Ken almost, but not quite, closed his eyes, pretending a drowsiness that he in no way felt. He watched through narrowed lids as Jess began slowly and lazily to undress, tossing each piece of clothing carelessly into a heap on the floor. His body came gradually into view, resplendent in its near-nakedness. Ken's throat was dry, and he felt himself trembling without knowing why. He had seen Jess in his shorts before, and even completely naked—at school in gym room showers, and on other occasions when they had spent the night together, and a couple of times they had gone skinny dipping together. But tonight was different. Tonight Jess would be in the same bed with him, that tall, husky body only inches away from him.

He closed his eyes finally, shutting out the view as Jess slipped off his trousers, circling the bed in his shorts to turn out the light. A minute later the bed sagged as he slipped under the sheet by Ken.

"You asleep?" Jess whispered into the darkness. His heart pounding, Ken said nothing, answering the question with a forced deepening of his breath. Those words—the same words his brother had used—his own brother. He had pretended to sleep that time too, not in the mood for conversation, not aware for several long minutes of the hand creeping across the bed, until it had reached him—his own brother! He had promised himself that it would not happen again, that it was only because they were sharing a bed on vacation, but it had happened again, and again, even after they were back to their twin beds, even when his brother had to steal from his bed in the dark, creep across the room....

118

THE *WHY NOT*, by Victor J. Banis

Suddenly, overpoweringly, Ken had an urge to reach out as his brother had reached out, move his hand across the bed, touch Jess' body. Jess was asleep already, his breathing deep and regular. It would be easy to move one hand, span the distance between them. Jess might not even wake up, and if he did...Ken pulled his hand, already sliding across the bed, back to his side. His heart was threatening to burst through the confines of his chest.

I'll only touch it, he thought, allowing his hand to move for an inch or so again. With a groan, he jerked it back, turned on his side, away from Jess. He felt as though he were on fire from the heat of Jess' body.

He moved as far away as possible, hugging the wall, trying to sleep, but to no avail. Finally, moving with painful caution to avoid waking Jess, he crawled out of the bed, over the foot of the bed so as not to touch Jess. In the light that filtered through the window, he saw Jess kick off the sheet. He had taken off his jockeys, too. He lay in the moonlight, his nakedness exposed to view. He was hard, even though he was asleep. It stood straight up.

For several long minutes Ken stood in the center of the room, telling himself to dress, to leave and go home. Then, wearily, he moved back toward the bed, his eyes riveted to the moonlight-streaked body that seemed to be drawing him on, like an all-powerful magnet.

He thought, as his hand reached out, of his brother, sleeping alone.

12:47 AM
Sunday Morning

◀Chapter Four▶

Dennis Lang nodded good night to Jackie and pushed his way through the *Why Not* crowd, through the drapes and out to the street beyond, drinking deep of the fresh night air after the clouds of cigarette smoke inside.

He stood for a moment, zipping up his jacket, and started off down the street in the direction of his apartment, eager to be home and comfortably in bed. There was not, in his case, any particular regret that he was going home alone. Shy, reserved, rather a private person, Dennis was usually alone and usually comfortable about it. There were, to be sure, those occasions such as this one when he wanted, for a brief time, to be among people. Invariably he would choose a place such as the Why Not, where he could be among many people, thus able to maintain, at the center of the storm as it were, his privacy and aloneness.

Such moods were usually of short duration, however, and after a beer or two he would leave and walk the few blocks back to his familiar, modest apartment, work the crossword puzzle from the paper or perhaps watch a late movie on television—the Lee Denver westerns were his favorites—before giving himself up to a pleasant night's sleep. He rarely had tricks and seldom felt the lack. He was not an unattractive young man but rather indifferent. Had he set his mind to it, he no doubt might have entertained any number of "guests," but his mind was rarely set to it.

This night, however, he had gone only a block before he noticed something slightly out of the ordinary. He glanced back as he started across the street, to discover that he was not alone. Behind him, perhaps a quarter of a block away, was another man whom he recognized as a customer of the *Why Not*. He had seen the man there on his way out, watching, it had seemed, his departure. As a rule he did not really notice the patrons of the bar but this one had been an exception, only in so much as he had been a rather conspicuous type—a little too adamantly masculine, a little too out-of-keeping. Surly, watchful, perhaps even resentful, and Dennis had concluded as he walked out of the bar that he was trade, rough trade, looking for money, or trouble, or both. But here he is, he thought uneasily, following me, without any encouragement or invitation. Maybe, he reminded himself, he is not following me at all. Maybe by mere coincidence he just chose to leave when I did.

Dennis turned the corner, walking a little more quickly down the darker and more isolated side street, and a moment later heard the sound of footsteps behind him. He was being followed, he was sure of it now.

As though to confirm his suspicions, the man behind him spoke, shattered the relative silence of the empty street. "Got a match?" he asked, his voice sharp, clear, demanding attention.

THE *WHY NOT*, by Victor J. Banis

Dennis thought of ignoring the question, wondering if his follower would be discouraged. He even thought of running but the athletic figure behind him could no doubt easily outrun him if he chose to do so. In the end, Dennis stopped, fumbling in his jacket for a book of matches, and handed them to the man as he walked up.

"Going home?" the man asked, studying Dennis' worried face in the flare of the match. When Dennis nodded wordlessly he asked, "Want some company?"

"I don't think so," Dennis answered, not wanting to sound antagonistic yet not wanting to encourage the advances either.

The stranger laughed, not at all a pleasant sound. "Don't be coy," he said, "I saw you look me over as you came out of the bar. Come on, I'll walk with you."

Dennis started to protest but the expression on the stranger's face only frightened him the more. Instead he turned and began to walk again, his fears mounting as the stranger fell in beside him, keeping pace. They were almost home now and Dennis was convinced that his companion was trade, or dirt, looking for kicks by beating up somebody. He had heard of such things. One or two of his friends had been worked over by just such men. It seemed that there should be something he could do but he could think of nothing.

They were at the steps now leading to the small apartment building, nothing more than a house the interior of which had been remodeled to provide a number of small but adequate apartments.

"I'm not allowed to have guests," Dennis declared boldly, pausing at the steps.

The stranger laughed again, glancing at the darkened windows of the house. "Look's to me like everybody is in bed for the night by this time. No one will know the difference."

"I don't think I want company," Dennis insisted, as firmly as he could manage. The stranger said nothing, only continued to stare at him with those cold, violent eyes and that ominous smile. Not sure whether he had discouraged the matter or not, Dennis turned quickly and started up the steps, wishing he could lock the street door behind him. His fear became genuine alarm as he realized the man was following him up the steps, into the hall.

Walking swiftly, almost running, Dennis hurried the length of the hall to his door. There was no one on the first floor who would be of any help to him. The landlord, he knew, was out of town for the weekend and the only other occupant was the old lady, Mrs. Beasley. Even if she were able to hear any disturbance, which was unlikely without her hearing aid, she would certainly be of no assistance.

He reached his door, unlocked it quickly and was almost able to get it closed before his pursuer reached it, thrusting his foot forcefully inside.

"You're not very sociable," he said, smiling all the while. He put one hand against the door, pushing it forcibly open. Shaking, Dennis stood stubbornly in the way, refusing to grant admittance. If anything was going to happen it was better to have it happen here in the hall where at least someone going by might see, although that was a slim chance at this hour, on this street.

THE *WHY NOT*, by Victor J. Banis

"Look, I'm tired," he argued, knowing that his voice was strained and unnaturally high. "If it's money you are after I'll give you what I have. It's only a couple of dollars but you are welcome to it."

The man chuckled, leaning slightly closer, and Dennis was painfully aware of the sheer bulk of him, brute force written across his countenance. "You know what I want, sugar; don't fool around with me. You were out after something and I have got it for you."

"No," Dennis shook his head, wanting to move back but afraid of granting admittance to the apartment.

"You weren't in that queer bar for nothing, sweetheart. Come on, take a look at what I got for you."

Dennis stared in frightened astonishment, unable to believe what was happening. The man was exposing himself, right here in the lighted hallway. He's crazy, Dennis told himself, the thought only adding to his fear.

"Come here," the man snapped. He caught Dennis' hand, pulling it toward him. Genuinely alarmed now, Dennis yanked his hand free, just as the front door opened. They both turned to see a stranger enter the hall and walk purposefully toward them.

"What's going on here?" he asked loudly, taking in the scene.

Almost overcome with relief, Dennis sobbed and stepped out into the hall. "Thank God you came by," he gasped. "This man...."

"This fairy is playing hard to get, Jack," the man beside him said. Dennis froze, his words jamming together in his throat. They knew each other. They were together.

"One of them cute ones," the second man said, standing beside them now.

"I...." Dennis tried to say but the newcomer cut him off.

"Save it, sister," he said. He flashed his open wallet in Dennis' face.

Police! Vice officers! But he hadn't done anything. They couldn't molest somebody like common thugs and then arrest you as though you had done something wrong.

"Come on," the newcomer ordered, taking his arm roughly, bringing a gasp of pain from Dennis' throat. They were arresting him; they were going to take him away. "But I haven't...." he tried to protest.

"Hey," the first one said, addressing his friend as though Dennis were unworthy of a comment, "What's the rush? This little faggot's been giving me a rough time, being real cute. What do you say, let's cool him down a little before we take him in, okay?"

The suggestion seemed to amuse his companion. Dennis felt a cold chill move slowly up the length of his spine. They were looking at him now with new, even more frightening expressions, holding him firmly in their grip. He shook his head, struggling to pull free from them, but there were two of them and they were too strong for him. They pulled him backward, into the apartment, and there was no doubt of what they intended to do. The door closed behind them.

THE *WHY NOT*, by Victor J. Banis

He opened his mouth to scream but a massive fish crashed into his jaw, jarring his head violently backward and he tasted the salty warmth of blood in his mouth. He began to cry, sobbing and pleading incoherently with them as they threw him across the bed. Too frightened to struggle, barely conscious of what was happening, he was dimly aware of hands everywhere—covering his mouth, pinning his arms down, roughly ripping the trousers from his body. His face was crushed into a pillow; the weight of a body falling across his drove the breath from him. A sudden scorching pain all but made him faint.

He struggled then, weakly, trying to move away from the pressing body, but there was no escape from the driving pain. It reached an unbearable peak. The hands of the man above him, hands coarse with thick, black hair, gripped his naked hips brutally.

Later, much later, he was aware of being led from the building—dragged, really—and shoved rudely into a car outside.

"They can't do this," he told himself over and over again, numbly. But they were doing it and he was helpless to stop it. It was his word against theirs; that was what they had warned him. Two of them. And anybody could find out, if they took the trouble to check, that he was gay. Anyone would believe that he had cruised them, made advances as they had said. And they had warned him what would happen to him if he even tried to contradict him.

"You think we were rough that time, we can be a lot rougher," one of them had told him ominously. "You don't want to find out."

THE *WHY NOT*, by Victor J. Banis

He began to sob, hopelessly, despairingly, wishing that he were dead.

****

Lynn saw Dave the minute he entered the doorway, holding the drapes boldly apart as he came through them. He waved, catching Dave's searching eye, and smiled with unconcealed pleasure as his friend made his way through the crowd to the table in the corner.

"Have any trouble finding the place?" he asked as Dave seated himself, stretching his long legs out to the side. He looks good, Lynn thought; he looks just as good as ever.

Dave shook his head, returning the same delighted smile, although in his expression there was a trifle of something else, a concern that became more apparent as he glanced again around the room.

"Do you come here often?" he asked, still looking about the crowded bar. Lynn blushed, glancing down at the floor.

"No, I've only been here once before." That was not true, but a fairly harmless lie. "It was the only place I could think of to tell you to meet me." That sounded silly, he thought uncomfortably. There were all sorts of places two people could meet: the bus station, a street corner. In truth, he had not really thought about Dave's reaction to the *Why Not*. Why should he object, after all, after what had been between them? True, they had never discussed it, but it had been there, you couldn't pretend it hadn't.

THE *WHY NOT*, by Victor J. Banis

Dave seemed to have accepted the answer, however, as logical. When he looked back, he had dismissed the concern and was once again the friend from their common past. "How long have you been in town?"

"Two weeks. I didn't know you were here until my mother sent your address in her last letter. She said nothing about you, though, or what you were doing here. How are you, anyway?"

"Never been better." Dave instinctively pulled his shoulders back. "How about you? You look great after all these years."

It has been years, hasn't it? Lynn thought, aware of the frequent glances in their direction. What was it about Dave? He was not the best looking man in the world, not even a sensational body. His hips had always been a little too wide, his legs too long for the rest of him. But there was something, something that seemed to appeal especially to the sort of men in this room. The unattainable air? A mysterious difference? Dave *was* different. In the room filled with men of every sort and description, he stood out like a sore thumb, only nicely so. Out of place here and yet, among the dozens of out-of-place individuals, he looked somehow more at home than any of them, with a certain naturalness about him that would have made him seem right for any setting.

"I've missed you," Lynn said abruptly, interrupting their stream of small talk. Dave smiled, that strange smile that told nothing.

"It's good to see you again, too" Dave said, noncommittally.

"Have you been happy?" Lynn pursued, hoping desperately to gain some comment more definitive, more intimate. After all, they were intimate—had *been* intimate. They deserved more from one another than small talk.

"I'm married, you know," Dave said, and his voice was slightly louder, more decisive. Lynn didn't know, of course, and Dave would know that he didn't.

"Anyone I know?" Lynn asked finally, wanting to sound pleased and aware that he had failed. Dave, married? No one had told him. But then, he had been so out of touch with everyone at home....

"Lettie. Lettie Mason."

Lynn caught his breath, embarrassed at once by his obvious consternation. Lettie—of course, she and Dave had often been together, friends through school—but, married? Lettie Mason, a black girl?

"How nice." It was the only thing he could think of to say. The air of warm cordiality between them had vanished, to be replaced by something colder, unnatural. "Did she object to your coming out tonight, to see me?"

Dave relaxed again, but not so much as before, rather as though he were making an effort to restore their good moods. "No," he said, shaking his head. "She asked if I would rather bring you by the apartment but I told her we would just bore her to tears, two old school buddies yakking about old times together. I will have to leave soon, though. I came on a bus."

Had that been the real reason? Or had Dave also wanted them to be alone together? "I'll drive you back," Lynn offered quickly, eager for the

130

chance to be away from the crowd in the bar, if only in the not-too-private interior of a car. "We can go now, if you like."

Dave glanced around. He had not yet even ordered a drink for himself. He dismissed that idea though and nodded. "Sure," he said, "We can talk better in the car anyway."

But they didn't talk any better in the car. Whatever their reunion had aroused in them, it was gone and they were like strangers now, careful of what they said, both too eager to be pleasing and interesting, both too mindful of the years that lay between them. Lynn had begun to feel the telltale warnings of a headache by the time he pulled up to the curb in front of the apartment house Dave indicated. Not a very nice-looking building, and an even less impressive neighborhood. But then, a white man with a Negro wife....

"Would you like to come in?" Dave asked, giving him that forlorn look that Lynn remembered so well. For an instant he almost accepted.

"No, I had better not," he decided aloud.

Dave shrugged, reaching for the door handle. "I guess the kid is probably asleep by now anyway. Lettie wouldn't want me waking him up."

"You have a baby?" Lynn asked, surprised by this additional news.

"Didn't I tell you that? But he's not a baby any more; almost two."

Lynn wanted to ask if the baby were white or black. "How nice," he said again.

Dave reached once more for the door handle, winced, and raised one hand to his shoulder.

THE *WHY NOT*, by Victor J. Banis

"What's wrong with your shoulder?" Lynn asked.

"Oh, I pulled a muscle lifting some furniture last week. It's still sore from it."

Lynn's voice was unsteady as he asked, "Would you like me to rub it for you?"

That was how it had all started for them: a sore shoulder from football; a rubdown, that went down, and down, until the shoulder had been forgotten in the exploration of the new interests they had discovered together.

"No, that's too much trouble," Dave insisted, but he had taken his hand from the door handle and he sounded anything but firm in his reply.

"Don't be silly. I used to be pretty good at making you feel better," Lynn argued, moving slightly across the seat. "Turn around where I can reach it."

Dutifully, pleased by the attention, Dave turned, facing out of the car. He sighed as Lynn's surprisingly strong hands began to massage the muscles of his back, stroking, rubbing, pulling.

Lynn's breath was rapid and strained, his own body rigid with tension. He could close his eyes and sketch this back, identify it from thousands of others. How often he had remembered it, dreamed of his hands again moving over its surface. He wanted to ask Dave to remove his shirt, but thought better of it.

They sat in silence, broken by an occasional grunt of pleasure from Dave. Lynn's hands moved automatically, making their way downward, upward, over the rippling muscles of the arms, kneading the back of the neck, down again, to the waist

132

this time, up the spine, over the shoulders, back to the waist, moving still lower. He held the familiar hips in his hands, followed the curve of the buttocks to the seat itself—in his imagination he touched naked flesh with his fingers.

"I guess I had better go in," Dave said abruptly, breaking the spell between them as he pulled quickly away.

Startled and annoyed, Lynn tried to sound light and unconcerned, reaching again for the beloved body. "Don't be silly. You're still stiff as a board. I don't know how...."

Dave had turned toward him and in the dim glow of light from the dashboard Lynn could see the mound of flesh pushing against the fabric of Dave's jeans, fighting to be free of its confinement. Dave was aroused. He too had remembered the massages of the past and his body had responded to the long-ago-instilled habit.

"Don't go," Lynn said, his voice pleading and urgent. He wanted to reach out, grasp the familiar bulge in his hand, but Dave was opening the door, slipping out of the car and away from him.

"Lettie says I am to ask you for dinner some night," Dave told him, crouching down to look through the doorway at Lynn. Lynn nodded sadly, unable to keep his eyes from the assertive hardness still all too apparent.

"Give me a call," he answered. He watched as Dave turned and walked hurriedly up the steps toward the house, pausing at the door for an identifiable gesture of rearrangement.

Lynn lifted his eyes, met his own gaze in the rear view mirror of the car. With a dismal smile he moved, slid under the wheel of the car and drove slowly away from the curb.

There was still time to return to the *Why Not*, time for another drink. Maybe even time to meet a new friend.

* * * * * * *

The nearest parking space that Lon could find was three blocks away from the *Why Not*, a fact that did not do anything to alleviate his bad spirits. He sat for a few minutes in the car. It was already after one, but he wanted Jackie to worry—not that Jackie really would worry.

It was not that he objected to gay bars. He went to them himself from time to time, but not the really wild ones, like the *Why Not*. He went to those with shows—some of the shows were surprisingly good—or he went to one of the better class ones, usually to meet one of the friends he had made in the Navy. He cultivated friendships, preserved them. But the *Why Not* represented everything that he disliked about gay bars—screaming faggots, drag queens, rough trade—it was cheap and tawdry and, probably as much because of those qualities as anything, successful.

Impatient after all to see Jackie, he left the car and walked toward the bar. He was cruised three times on the way, by passing motorists, no doubt on their way to the *Why Not* and seeking parking places. He ignored them, and stepped through the curtained doorway.

The bar was jammed, as was to be expected on a Saturday night. He shouldered his way through the crowd, feeling a combination of furtive pleasure and annoyance as a hand grasped at his crotch and squeezed quickly.

It was a full five minutes before Jackie noticed him and hurried down to the end of the bar where he was standing. In the meantime he was not really alone. A rather handsome young man, looking more like a college athlete than a customer for a gay bar, stood beside him, brazenly examining the tall newcomer with obvious interest.

"All by your lonesome?" college boy asked.

"Not much longer," Lon told him as Jackie approached.

The stranger glanced from Lon to Jackie and sighed. "I might have known," he commented dryly. "That one always gets the cream of the crop—so to speak." He moved away, disappearing into the crowd.

"Just in the nick of time," Lon announced as Jackie set a drink in front of him. "I almost had a new playmate."

"He's lousy in bed—that's what I've heard, anyway."

"I'll bet I wouldn't have to wait all night to see him alone."

"Oh, don't be a drag," Jackie hissed, turning away to wait on a customer.

Lon waited quietly, sipping his drink, while Jackie hurried to and fro, attending to the wants of others along the bar. Lindy came by once and mumbled a not-too-friendly greeting.

"You know," Lon said to him, unable to resist a bit of maliciousness, "If I didn't know better I would guess that you are jealous."

THE *WHY NOT*, by Victor J. Banis

"Of you and Jackie?" Lindy did not look up from the drinks he was pouring. "Maybe you would be right." He left before the conversation could be pursued further.

Lon smiled, wondering how much longer the status quo would remain. His eyes followed Jackie's lithe body, in rapid motion behind the bar. The turtleneck jersey and the denim stretch pants accentuated the austere thinness of the figure, adding to the illusion of extreme youth. Jackie bent, buttocks thrust ungracefully into the air. Lon smiled and grew more impatient for the time to pass.

* * * * * * *

Furtively, stealthily, the shadowy figures dart from the street, moving quickly through the area of light near the motel office, taking the steps two at a time. Scrambling over themselves and one another, they glide into the room and Don closes the door behind them, glancing first in the direction of the lighted window of the office.

The sailors are laughing now, breathlessly, excited, talking in little whispers to one another. Terry listened instinctively—their words, spoken in Greek, indistinguishable to him—yet hoping to determine in their tone and inflection a clue to—to what? So much to wonder about, so much he did not know. Are they safe, really interested in a few minutes of fun with some American boys, or rough trade, looking for violence, or perhaps just some money? Hard to imagine, they have been so sweet up till now. Who was it they said he looked like:

THE *WHY NOT*, by Victor J. Banis

Brigitte Bardot's husband? Terry makes a mental note to find a picture of his alleged look-alike.

They are all here now, in the one room, in the motel, after driving for an hour looking for a spot, the Greek sailors growing more restless, more insistent in their gestures, squeezing Terry's bottom, making their desires all too clear. I don't like it that way, Terry reminds himself, remembering clearly the pain he had experienced on the last attempt; but they are nice, these Greek sailors, chivalrous, romantic, saying the sweetest things—or rather, one of them saying the sweetest things for the others, the only one who speaks English, and he is far from skilled in the tongue.

It is the one who speaks English who is interested in Terry, which is not to Terry's liking, for one of the others is cuter—a real doll, slim and young, terribly young—a virgin, the English-speaker tells them, who has never had a boy. Terry wants desperately to be the first, but Don has beaten him to it, already has claimed the pretty one for himself—Aris, was that the name? Hard to tell in that broken English.

"It's going to be crowded in here," Terry comments, glancing at the one double bed. He dislikes that sort of thing, group activities. He has decided to give Don the bed, confine himself to the floor, which is at least carpeted. He will put a blanket down, that should suffice.

"Plenty of room," Don assures him, already undressing. The sailors have taken their cue from him and are peeling their uniforms from their lithe young bodies. Shy, wishing that the light were off, Terry begins to undress also, stripping down to his

137

shorts. Then, suddenly embarrassed by the sight of nude bodies all around him—Don is already on the bed, reaching for the light with one hand, Aris with the other—Terry excuses himself and hurries into the bathroom, closing the door behind himself. He runs the water, decides impulsively to shower, and reaches in to start the shower running before he slips his shorts down over his hips, stepping out of them. The door opens, startling him, and the English-speaking sailor—John, he thinks—comes in, naked, his oily flesh gleaming in the bright light.

"I was going to take a shower," Terry explains, speaking slowly and distinctly, watching the smiling face to see if he has been understood. Whether he understands or not, the sailor has other ideas. He takes Terry into his arms, pulling him close. Terry tilts his face, expecting a kiss, but the dark face pulls away. He isn't going *that* far. Resigned but not discouraged, Terry yields willingly to the hands that guide him downward, pulling him to the floor. The tile is cold, broken only by the small area of bath mat and Terry wishes again that the lights were out, but the Greek is impatient, too eager to bother with such niceties.

Terry groans but he lies still as the Greek advances. Then, eager to please this dark, hungry man, and thrilled despite the unfamiliar act, Terry responds, arching his back, twisting, writhing. Strong hands cling to him, the breath is rapid and fervent in his ear, building to a smothered shout.

Later, the Greek motions for Terry to remain there. He brings a damp towel and tenderly wipes Terry clean, his hands astonishingly gentle. He gives Terry an affectionate pat on the shoulder and leaves.

Dazed, pleased despite the pain, Terry stands, steps into the shower and begins to soap himself. But he is not alone for long. The curtain parts—he hasn't heard the door—and another one enters. The young one, the beautiful one. He smiles at Terry, bashful but radiant—Don has done a good job, it seems—and takes the other bar of soap, begins to wash himself. Shyly he hands the soap to Terry and Terry obediently begins to wash the hard young body.

Terry kneels, oblivious to the water rushing down upon his head. The beautiful young body arches toward him. But Don has done too good a job it seems. Embarrassed by his own failure, the youth blushes, laughs and shrugs apologetically. Terry laughs with him, graciously washes the boy's back.

Brought together by their mutual embarrassment, they come out of the shower and towel each other dry, watching themselves in the long mirror on one wall. Terry wishes that they might remain together, he and this laughing, comfortable youth beside him. So warm, so pleasant, so different from the other young men, countless men, who have been intimate with him in the past.

Don enters, wanting the bathroom, and they give it to him, exchanging rooms. The third sailor joins Don in the bathroom and Terry and the other two begin to dress, slowly, regretfully. They, the Greeks, must return to their ship soon. They smoke cigarettes, trying to talk, the one interpreting for the other. Finally Don and the third sailor come out of the bathroom, begin also to dress.

THE *WHY NOT*, by Victor J. Banis

Soon, all too soon, it is time to go. Don returns to the bathroom to use the toilet and Terry stands with his three new friends, smiling lingeringly at them. Aris takes his hands, returns his smile with an element of sadness in his expression. Then, growing frivolous again, for he is too young to remain long serious, he takes Terry's waist in his strong young hands and lifts Terry upward, over his head to the ceiling, proud of his strength and showing off, and an affectionate, a playful gesture as well. He lowers Terry gently to the surface of the bed and they embrace. He wants, Terry thinks, to try again. He is rested now, ready to finish what they were unable to accomplish in the shower.

But Don has come back, reminding them of the time, and they get up from the bed, shake hands all around in an oddly formal gesture, before stealing one at a time, out the door and hurrying back to the car.

So early, Terry thinks, bringing up the rear—too early. But the Greek navy, the sailors tell them, is very strict. Perhaps, when they have driven these young men to their ship, perhaps he and Don will have time for a drink at the *Why Not*.

I am drinking too much, Freddie warned himself, holding his empty glass in the air to catch Lindy's attention. Lindy nodded, stretched over the crowd of heads at the bar and took the glass, handing it back a minute later again full. Freddie dropped some change into the outstretched hand and returned his attention to the crowded room. Try though he might he just couldn't get awfully interested in anything present. He just wasn't with it. He

140

was still annoyed with the way the day had gone and particularly with Walt—moving, just walking out on him, leaving him to sink or swim.

Even Walt's gracious offer to come with him to the bar tonight had not really smoothed over the troubled waters. Not that Walt was much company anyway, standing all by himself at the cigarette machine, like a wooden Indian. He should mingle, Freddie decided, and almost marched across the room to say so, but then he thought better of it. It would only annoy Walt and cause more friction.

If only Walt would find someone, a new lover. Their own relationship was far in the past, too far to be recalled. Walt owed it to himself to find someone. But that, regrettably, Freddie reminded himself, still left him out in the cold—just where I am anyway, he thought dismally.

Without checking the time, he knew it was late. People were matching up with less selectiveness, taking what they could get before the evening came to an end. Good God, am I going to end up without anything, he thought with alarm? Ridiculous, to come here, spend all that money on drinks, and end up sleeping alone.

He smiled as a familiar face moved toward him in the dim light, returned Bert's greeting without any great feeling of pleasure or dislike. "I thought you would be dashing off with someone by this time," Freddie commented, moving slightly sideways to allow Bert room to stand beside him.

"Oh, they are all so dull tonight," Bert replied drearily, his expression appallingly bored.

THE *WHY NOT*, by Victor J. Banis

At his gesture Jackie appeared with a fresh drink. "If they are so dull, why do you bother?" Jackie asked.

A good question, Freddie thought, taking another hearty swallow from his own drink—why do we bother?

"Sometimes I wonder about that one," Bert commented, nodding after Jackie's retreating figure.

"Jackie? Nothing to wonder about," Freddie said. "Jackie likes two sexes, men and boys."

The conversation died for a moment. "I like your friend," Freddie commented. He nodded in the direction of the little group Bert had just left—four or five fellows standing together, talking superficially while they cruised.

"Do you?" Bert asked, mildly surprised. "As a matter of fact, that's why I'm here—to find out if you are interested. He wanted to know."

Freddie felt the familiar tingling in the stomach, a flutter of excitement, but it was replaced almost at once by feeling of annoyance. If he is so interested, why doesn't he come over here himself instead of sending a messenger?

"I might be," he decided aloud, wondering as he glanced again in that direction and caught a quick smile, just how interested this friend was. Interested enough to persist? "I might be."

Bert shrugged, drifted away soon to rejoin his group. Freddie saw him speak to his friend. Oh, please, he thought fervently, please come over, speak to me. Already he was regretting being coy, wondering if he should join the group after all and make his interest known. He caught another glance and felt some relief. He was interested after all. He would come over soon.

Not wanting to be too obvious, Freddie turned his head, studied the faces around him, many of them familiar, all of them repetitious. No, Bert's friend was, without a doubt, the best thing in the room. He glanced back and his mouth fell open. His would-be suitor had indeed left the little group he had been socializing with, but he was standing at the bar, talking to someone else. A swishy little fairy, Freddie decided, not the friend's type at all, he felt positive. He'll come back to me after all.

He watched the two, talking and laughing with one another and realized with some fright that it was growing very late. They would be calling the last call soon, sending everyone home, and there he stood, that silly man, wasting his time with that giddy faggot, when I am standing here by myself, waiting for him to come over and talk to me.

They can't be, he thought suddenly—but they were; the two of them were getting ready to leave together. The dark one helping the little queen into her sweater. And there they went, toward the door. For a fleeting instant at the door the dark one glanced back and then he was gone and Freddie was left alone, a half-finished drink in his hand.

* * * * * * *

Jack Leeds passed the entrance to the *Why Not*, walking, without being aware of the fact, slightly faster until he had reached the corner beyond. Consciously, Jack was not unkind in his attitudes toward the young men who came and went through the open doorway. He had the sophisticate's knowledge of such things and a genuine sympathy for his fellow men, sexual proclivities notwithstanding. In reality he did not often even think of these people, except on such occasions as this, when his route home took him past the noise and the activity of the *Why Not*.

His indifference, unlike that of many heterosexuals with whom he was acquainted, was genuine. If there was any such leaning in his make-up, and he was studied enough to know that it was possible, it was well below the conscious level of his awareness, a latent possibility at best; that had not, in his thirty-seven years been tapped and was not very likely to be. He was, in his own thinking, a man, confident and sure of his masculinity and thus with no need to establish the fact to anyone else's satisfaction.

The intrusion of the *Why Not*'s wee hours frivolity behind him, he resumed his slower pace, enjoying, as he always did, the late night isolation of his walk. He neared Santa Monica Boulevard, turned the corner, and reached his bus stop. Sometimes, if he felt particularly energetic, he would walk the additional two miles to his home, enjoying the opportunity to exert himself physically, eager for the contented sleep that would follow. But tonight the sleep would be delayed and there would be better uses for his energies. Susan would be there, waiting for him at the apartment, fresh coffee made and waiting for him in the kitchen, a record on the phonograph waiting to be switched on as he unlocked the door.

THE *WHY NOT*, by Victor J. Banis

He thought of Susan with a pleasant, warm feeling. How long had it been now, a year? She was a good woman, in the best sense of the term, comfortable to be around, nice to hold against him in the still darkness of the late night hours.

Tonight—maybe tonight he would do what he had been considering for several months: ask her to marry him. It would make her happy, that much he knew, although he loved her the more for never bringing the matter up, or trying to change the status quo between them. Susan was, *sans doute*, the marrying kind. He had known that from their first meeting, but she had offered no prolonged resistance to his advances and she had fitted herself willingly to his schedule, his personality, his independence. She had been happy to accept whatever he gave and had proved herself worthy of more. Maybe, just maybe....

The headlights of a car approached slowly down the street, driving close to the curb. For a moment Jack was unable to define the uneasiness that he felt; then, studying the car as it came nearer, he realized that the car had passed him before, a moment ago, turning the corner beside him. It had come around the block apparently, approaching him slowly, closer to the curb where he stood than was ordinary.

His first thought was that he was about to be propositioned, not an unusual occurrence for someone of his physical merits, and he prepared himself without bitterness but with firmness to decline the invitation.

He knew however as the car pulled alongside him that he had been mistaken in that assumption.

THE *WHY NOT*, by Victor J. Banis

The five or six young toughs in the car were not planning to proposition him, he was certain of that. It was trouble, maybe. A gang of kids riding around town and looking for trouble.

The car stopped and the passenger closest to him, a swarthy-looking young man with bad teeth, leaned out the open window. "You come from the *Why Not?*" he asked, smiling a rather lewd smile.

Unfrightened, a little angry, Jack shook his head. "No, as a matter of fact, I didn't," he answered in a clear, firm voice. He thought, after he had said it, that it would have been wiser to pretend that he did not know the name of the bar. Recognition might well be construed as an admission of guilt. That thought, however, only added fuel to his annoyance—as though he need explain or apologize to a bunch of punk kids.

The passenger repeated his answer to the others in the car and there was some conversation among them, most of which Jack did not hear. One of them however decided in a louder voice than the others that he was lying.

"Don't kid us, Ace," the passenger said, speaking to him again. "How about a lift?"

"No, thanks," Jack answered him, glancing down the street in the direction his bus would come. There were no other cars out just now; the street was empty. There were six of them in the car; he had counted them in the interval. He might have his hands full if they really wanted to make trouble.

"He doesn't like us," the boy told his companions in a falsetto voice. Then, turning back to Jack, "Hey, we're all right, sweetheart. We'll give you a good time."

146

THE *WHY NOT*, by Victor J. Banis

Jack remained where he was, continuing to look up the street and trying to ignore them. They sat for a moment longer, then, to his relief, pulled away. His relief was short lived. They pulled into the lot behind him and started getting out of the car.

He stood frozen, tensed for action as the young men approached him, forming a loose circle about him. "What's the matter, sweetie," one of them asked, "You don't like us?"

Jack remained silent. He could tell them that they had made a mistake, show them the wedding band on his left hand. He wouldn't have to tell them how many years his wife had been dead.

"You are gay, aren't you?" another one asked, placing himself directly in front of Jack, so close that Jack could see his own reflection in the cold, staring eyes. He held his lips firmly shut. Queer-hunting; he had heard of this sort of thing. Who did they think they were, running around looking for some poor fairy to scare the pants off? He had already determined that he would not give them the satisfaction of telling them they were mistaken.

"Hey, he spoke to you!" One of the kids grabbed the lapel of his jacket, yanking Jack around. Angry, too angry to think, Jack struck out with his fist, catching the kid on the chin. It was the spark that touched off the brooding violence about him. "You dirty son-of-a-bitch," he heard and then they were on him, kicking, slugging, dragging him down.

He fought back, fought well and hard, but there were too many of them for him. Bastards, he swore silently, fighting now for his life. He knocked one of them down, brought his knee up into the crotch of another one.

THE *WHY NOT*, by Victor J. Banis

He saw the tire iron in the one boy's hand but he couldn't shake the two on top of him, strong arms holding him, pinning his own arms to his side. With a frantic burst of strength he turned, dragging them with him, but he was too late. The world seemed to explode about him as the iron struck his skull, crushing the bone. He sank to the ground, unaware of the second and third blows, never to be aware of anything again.

Headlights appeared in the distance and the youths dashed for their car, left in a roar and a squeal of tires. Sprawled across the sidewalk behind them, Jack Leeds lay dead.

THE *WHY NOT*, by Victor J. Banis

1:50 AM
Sunday Morning

◀Chapter Five▶

Instinct warns that the time is drawing to an end. No need to check watches or ask the hour, for all those here know, sense in the mounting, breathless tempo, that it is almost over. The glances have become maddeningly more frantic, the movements quicker, the drinks disappearing with ever-increasing rapidity. Dates are made, partners chosen, parties planned for after hours. A few have darted away, afraid to face the inevitable climax of their efforts, but most remain, scurrying about, desperately hopeful even at that late stage in the game.

A warning voice cries "last call," the alarm from Jackie sounding through the dismal night, and then a shock wave as the lights come on, glaring mercilessly, aging those powdered figures who have worked so hard to be young, shattering illusions and spirits. Bloodshot eyes blink, reexamine nearby faces. Some change their minds, pretend to be too drunk, and stagger away alone rather than fulfill their impetuous commitments. Others are pleasantly surprised, relieved that the darkness did not flatter out of proportion.

A desolate wasteland of emptied glasses, emptied souls, the bar begins to empty, the *Why Not* settling herself slowly into the sawdust and dirt on her floor, ready now for rest and solitude. She has done her work for the night, this aged and vulgar Queen, given her show, danced her dance, made friends of strangers and strangers of friends, poured her wine and sung her sons. Off with you, she grumbles, leave me to my sorry rest.

She groans as the feet pass over her, licks her wounds and sighs a mother's sigh. How thoughtless children are, this mother-to-them-all murmurs, and her curtains flutter limply after the departing bodies, her door opening and closing with a tired rhythm. A cigarette smolders on the floor, a spilled drink sends its stale fluid trickling through the sawdust.

Outside, a lone sailor, lost perhaps, drifts slowly by, carried along by the floating street, glancing without interest at the darkened bar. He rounds a corner, disappears, and the *Why Not* folds in upon herself, tired, alone, whimpering softly in the night.

* * * * * * *

Bob listened with one ear to the conversation on his right, someone describing in tedious detail the plot, or lack of plot, to some book he had read. With the other half of his attention, Bob followed the noises from the hall, identifying the newcomers by their voices and the stream of conversation that preceded them down the hall toward the living room.

"I should go home," he told himself, swooshing his beer around in its can. He thought of his apartment, quiet, empty. It would be cold without Andy in it, and he decided to stay another hour. Andy would be home soon after that, his work finished for the night, and for the week. Next week Andy would be on days again and there would be no need to stay away from the apartment to escape the harsh loneliness that moved in to take Andy's place.

Agatha and Clara burst into the room, carrying sacks of beer and shouting their greeting at those already there. "Mercy, I don't know how you girls can dash away so early," Agatha exclaimed, handing her beer to the hostess. Tina scurried away to the kitchen with the sack, Clara following after her.

"I simply have to linger and see who makes out with who," Agatha went on, all the while examining the contents of the room.

"Whom," someone corrected her from the sofa.

"Don't you get fruity-snooty with me," Agatha shrieked, turning her evil eye on the speaker. "The only reason you left was because you didn't make out. And you know who that one left with, the little one you were eyeing? Some Mexican queen who hadn't combed her hair since the Frisco quake." This produced a burst of laughter and Agatha beamed proudly, happy to have established herself as a star of the evening.

Bob glanced again at his watch: it was just two thirty. The party was only beginning, a typical after-hours affair that would last well into the following morning, the guests plodding onward into the night, trying to convince themselves that they were having fun and ignoring the sad complaints of their weary bodies.

Andy, my Andy, he thought wearily, wishing again that his lover were with him. He yawned and rose, and moved toward the kitchen and a fresh beer.

The tempo had increased when he returned. Tina, the hostess, had created a makeshift gown for herself from a tattered bedspread and was loudly aping Scarlett O'Hara in an exaggerated Southern accent. "There I was, fleeing from the Yahnkees, Ashley off to the wars, Rhett had done left me, Miss Melohnee in the back of the wagon birthing her baby—and the damned mule died!"

Someone else had come in, a pair of queens unknown to Bob, jabbering loudly about a gang of dirt outside. "Lovely little things," one of them crooned. "But so nasty. One of them told Maggie to bare her ass, right there on the steps."

The laugher that followed the tale was tinged with a sprinkling of uneasiness—dirt, trouble, lingering outside. Seating himself again at the sofa, Bob wondered if he should leave after all, just in case. For Andy's sake if not for his own. Andy could not afford to be mixed up in any trouble.

But, if he left now, he would have to pass right by the gang hanging around outside, and that could be difficult. And there were more people arriving now, more voices from the hall, and he lingered a little longer—too long, as it turned out, for in a moment the voices in the hall changed, the room suddenly became tense, and a thin little man dashed into the room to announce that the dirt were in the house, virtually forcing their way inside.

There was a frenzy of squeals and screams, some very unladylike oaths, and a cloud of men, Levis, leather jackets, gleaming eyes, burst into the room, one of them dragging a bald auntie with him

154

THE *WHY NOT*, by Victor J. Banis

"Well, I'll be," one of them shouted to his companion, "If it isn't fairy-land."

Bob moved backward, reaching the relative safety of a doorway. He wanted fervently to leave but the escape was cut off by the young hoods—a dozen of them, maybe more, spilling into the room. The bedlam was growing, the toughs picking up ashtrays and bottles from the table to smash them on the floor, one of them slapping a frightened queen across the face. The queens were screaming and running about, shouting to one another and the boys, trying to get past the intruders to escape. Bob clamped a hand over his mouth, thinking that he was going to be sick.

The excitement reached a maddening peak and came to a sudden standstill as someone shouted, "It's the Law!"

Queens and dirt alike scattered, one of them kicking a glass from a window to escape from a bedroom, but there was too little time and not enough exits. A moment later the Law entered, dark-uniformed strangers, official, commanding, and the party died, fell limply at their feet.

"Well, thank God you got here," Tina declared, seemingly forgetful of the tattered bedspread and outlandish make-up he still wore. "I hope you caught some of those dreadful beasts."

"All right, what is this?" one of the officers, the sergeant apparently, demanded, glaring angrily about the room. He had already seen enough to tell him what kind of party it was and there was no sympathy in his eyes when he brought them to rest on Tina. "Who runs this place?"

THE *WHY NOT*, by Victor J. Banis

"It's my house," Tina bellowed defiantly, too angry to be frightened, "And I will not have a bunch of young punks crashing in here like that...."

"All right, sister, cool it," the officer told her, interrupting her rudely.

Still standing in the doorway at the end of the room, Bob had ceased to pay attention to their exchange, his attention focused instead on another of the officers, whose reflection faced him in the mirror. Their eyes met in the glass, a startled, despairing encounter. Bob felt a warning turn in his stomach. "I'm going to be sick," he told himself, fighting back the vile taste creeping into his mouth.

"You had better come with us," the first officer was saying to Tina. "All of you had better come with us."

"Well, of all the...." Tina sputtered, choking on his own words. "But didn't you see...?"

"I see a bunch of fairies disturbing the peace, that's what I see," he snapped, kicking at a piece of broken glass with one foot. "Take her with you, Andy," he told the officer near him. "We'll round up the rest of them."

In the mirror, Bob's eyes remained for another second on Andy's. "Andy, my Andy," he cried silently. "I won't be with you tonight."

* * * * * * *

Jackie stirred and reached toward the nightstand for a cigarette.

"You smoke too much," Lon growled.

156

THE *WHY NOT,* by Victor J. Banis

Jackie sighed and snuggled back against him, pressed close against the warm hardness of his body. For a moment they lay in comfortable silence.

"Lon?"

"Again?" His hand moved toward Jackie's thigh.

"Silly...." Jackie pushed Lon's hand away, but not too far away. "Have you ever thought about...well, about making an honest woman of me?"

"Sure. Lots of times," Lon said, "But I don't want to marry your brother too."

Jackie thought for a moment. "Lindy? You know, you are absolutely right. I mean, about my spoiling him so much. But he has done a lot for me, since the folks died. He saw to it that I got through school, and he's worked hard with the bar."

"And in the meantime he wraps you around his finger," Lon said. "Damn it, he has got no right to run your life the way he does. You're all grown up now."

"I know." Jackie patted the firm surface of his stomach. "But what I wanted to say was, it isn't just Lindy to be considered."

"Well, you're making sense for a change. It's about time you started thinking of you and me. Hell yes, I would love to have a wife and a few snot-nosed kids trailing around after me."

There was a moment of silence. "Would it really matter?" Jackie asked. "About the kids?"

"Matter? Sure. I'd like to be a father. Most guys do."

"I've been seeing Doctor Carter," Jackie said.

"You told me. If you're really thinking about any operations, the answer is no. I like you as a girl and I'll be damned if I want anything sewed on or whatever they do to make a man of you."

Jackie giggled nervously.

Lon suddenly jerked to a sitting position. "Hey, are you trying to tell me you're pregnant?" he asked, grinning. "That's great, you silly little...."

Jackie shook her head. "Not the slightest bit."

Lon reached for her. "Well, we can take care of that. God knows how we have missed connecting this long. I haven't been taking any precautions, you know that."

Jackie pushed his hand away nervously. "That's what I am trying to tell you, Lon. I haven't been taking any either."

Lon stared down at her for a moment. "What's that supposed to mean?" he asked.

Jackie reached for a cigarette again. This time Lon did not interfere, although he studied her coldly as she lit it.

"I am trying to explain," she said finally, exhaling loudly. "Lon, I have been *trying* to get pregnant. I haven't done anything either, and something should have happened long ago. That's why I went to see Doctor Carter. I thought I was doing something wrong. He even showed me ways to—well, ways to increase the chances."

"Maybe you're sterile." Lon said it simply but his voice had grown chilly.

Jackie shook her head again. "I was afraid of that. I had him check. The tests came out fine. I could get pregnant at the drop of a cell, only...."

"Only what?"

158

THE *WHY NOT*, by Victor J. Banis

Jackie reached for him but he stiffened at her touch and drew away from her.

She sighed and said it far more bluntly than she had intended. "The doctor says it must be you, you must be sterile."

"Like hell I am!" Lon snapped, jumping angrily from the bed. "If there is anything wrong, it's with you, sweetheart."

Jackie's heart sank. She had feared Lon's reaction to the suggestion—dear Lon, he was so butch, so masculine, so fearful of anything that threatened his all-male image.

"It wouldn't hurt you to have some tests," she argued without much hope of winning the point.

"I don't need some doctor to tell me that I'm a man," he shouted, pacing wildly back and forth across the room. "What do you think I am, one of those faggot friends of yours that you're always playing up to at the bar? You think I can't get a girl pregnant?"

"Have you? Have you ever gotten a girl pregnant?"

"How the hell should I know? Probably dozens of them, but most girls don't come running around publicizing the fact. Maybe they had it taken care of. Maybe they were careful not to let it happen. How should I know? That's for a woman to worry about."

"Lon...." Jackie was fighting back a wave of tears that was threatening to engulf her. It was going too far, too fast.

"Get out of here," he ordered her suddenly.

She stared at him, unable to believe what she had heard. It was plain from his expression though that she had not misunderstood him. He looked like a madman, his eyes flashing, his handsome features contorted with anger.

"Go on, beat it," he insisted. "You think I want to get married and then have to adopt kids? Have everybody laughing at me behind my back, saying I'm not man enough to make them on my own?"

His voice went on and on but Jackie ceased to listen to what he was saying. She felt tired and beaten down. Without a word she rolled from the bed, stood on the other side away from him and began to dress.

Lindy would be home by now. He would fuss at her about the hours she kept and make her eat something before she went to bed. Dear, sweet Lindy—he would make everything all right. He always did.

* * * * * * *

Late night now, another night at the *Why Not* ended, and this time no face to find on the morning pillow. Only a solitary walk, hurrying because it is cold, too cold for the thin sweater and the long walk home. Too late for buses and too broke for a cab. Walking quickly, past darkened windows and closed bars, alone on the sidewalk, although an occasional car passes on the street.

The aloneness is broken suddenly when a man appears—from where? —hurrying along behind. An old man, old and thin, a panhandler perhaps, walking fast, almost running to catch up to me. He'll want a dime for coffee and give me a hard-luck story that will probably coax some of the pitifully small change from my pocket. Alongside me now, trying breathlessly to keep pace, holding the too-thin coat tightly about himself in a vain attempt to be warm.

"Cold out tonight," he says, his eyes darting constantly to my face, seeking sympathy or perhaps another kind of warmth.

"Sure is," I agree, not wanting to be cruel, wishing he would walk ahead of me, or behind me.

"Could you use a couple dollars?" he asks me and I jump, caught off guard by the unexpected question, saying nothing while I try to organize my thoughts. "I'll give you two dollars," he goes on, speaking rapidly to deliver his message before I refuse or interrupt, "If you will let me do you. You know what I mean"

There it is, stripped of romance, void of excitement. The bottom line. Two dollars if you will let me do you. And I am tired, tired and cold.

"There isn't any place to go," I tell him meekly, touched by the desperate flicker in his eyes and the whine of his voice. I know that desperation. Only, I am still better equipped than he to satisfy it. For now. For a few years, at least. It occurs to me looking at him that I am seeing into the future. My future, perhaps.

"There's an alley—see, here," he tells me urgently, pointing to the darkened path leading from the relative light of the street into a pit of darkness, broken at its opposite end by another lighted street.

I say nothing, but my feet turn into the alley. We walk silently now and I am afraid. It is too public. Windows, black or not, might harbor watchers, a police car could pull into the alley, someone might pass by. No place to hide—only a shallow doorway which wouldn't begin to conceal even one of us.

"This is okay," he says, stopping at the doorway.

"Someone might come," I tell him but already he is at work, crouching on his knees on the hard, cold surface of the alley.

"It's okay," he tells me, hungrily taking the prize I offer. Even in the cold night air I am responding, and he gives himself up to his art, his acts not so much a matter of sex as of ritual, a ritual with which I am all too familiar. My legs spread tensely, I watch the streets at either end of the alley, feeling almost nothing from the area of his attention. His tongue caresses me, his mouth urgently demanding life from me.

The minutes seem like hours—too long, too long. I have had too much to drink, too much sex, too many hours of waking. Sorry for him, thinking him tired when he pauses, I start to move away, wanting to make it easier for him.

"No, please," he begs, clinging to me. "Let me, please."

On it goes until finally, with an immense relief, I feel the familiar surging in my groin. My legs, stiff from tension, tremble while his bony hands claw at my hips.

When it is over he is like a mother with her favorite child, tucking me gently away for the night.

Quickly, frightened at the boldness of what we have done, I fasten my trousers and we start together toward the street. He reaches for his wallet and I shake my head. "That's okay," I tell him, in some unfathomable way touched by him. "Forget the money."

"No, no, I want to," he insists, thrusting the two dollars into my hand, but not before I have seen that it leaves his billfold empty. I crumple the bills in my fist, shove them down into my pocket. At the street, we pause. He rests a hand upon my shoulder.

"You're a nice boy," he tells me, smiling faintly, and he is gone, vanishing once more into the night.

In my pocket my fingers touch the money again. Two dollars—enough, if I wanted to, to catch a cab.

ABOUT THE AUTHOR

*Lecturer, former writing instructor and early rab-
ble-rouser for gay rights and freedom of the press,
VICTOR J. BANIS is the critically acclaimed author
("...a master storyteller"—Publishers Weekly) of
more than 140 published novels and nonfiction
works, and his verse and short pieces have appeared in numerous journals (Blithe House Quar-
terly, Fall 2006) and anthologies (Charmed Lives,
Lethe Press, 2006).*